Praise for I'jaam

"Brief, bitter and bracing, I'jaam displays all the dangerous prismatic grace and light of shattered glass. Nuanced and direct, Antoon's razor-sharp voice rises out of the prisons and mass graves of Iraq during the era when Saddam Hussein enjoyed U.S. government support and no one heard these voices silenced in their tens and hundreds of thousands. The hopeful tenderness of this voice goes on speaking now, and we can be grateful that a new translation allows us, finally, to hear it. In this time of endless war, it tells (again) a story we needed so many lives ago."—Sesshu Foster, author of *Atomik Aztex* and *City Terrace Field Manual*

"Sinan Antoon's I'Jaam is a stunning work, as it brings to the present a world of terror we know about, we have previously read about, but which usually seems remote, unreal. It takes a great talent to make it so specific, so Iraqi in this case, and so personal. This author shows the particular sadistic humor that goes with cruelty, a "cultural" slant that makes us identify it with the places where it happens. Evil becomes thus both general, universal, and particular. The nightmare gains familiarity, reality."—Etel Adnan, author of *Sitt Marie Rose* and *In the Heart of the Heart of Another Country*

"Sinan Antoon's novel traces, across time, space and faces, how the life of a young generation under a barbaric regime becomes an existential minefield. Life is no more what it is. Everything is a trace of itself. Even daily language is cluttered with debris from the mines of hell. Incessantly targeted in a nightmarish atmosphere, the individual can only save him/herself with the stubbornness of an animal."—Saadi Youssef, author of *Without an Alphabet, Without a Face: Selected Poems*

"Sinan Antoon writes with an assurance of voice, a clear redefinition of form and narrative, and compelling and beautiful language. Iraqi in origin, but global in its scope, this book is deeply human." — Chris Abani, author of *The Virgin of Flames* and *GraceLand*

I'jaam

an iraqi rhapsody

SINAN ANTOON

Translated by Rebecca C. Johnson and Sinan Antoon

With an Introduction by Elias Khoury

CITY**LIGHTS**
SAN FRANCISCO

Cover image by Muhammad Saad al Shammarey
Cover design by Yolanda Montijo
Book design by Elaine Katzenberger
Typesetting by Harvest Graphics

An excerpt from *I'jaam* was published in *Banipal: Magazine of Modern Arab Literature*, No. 19, Spring 2004.

Library of Congress Cataloging-in-Publication Data

Antoon, Sinan, 1967–
  [I'jaam. English]
  I'jaam : an Iraqi rhapsody / by Sinan Antoon ; translated by Rebecca Johnson and Sinan Antoon.
     p.   cm.
  ISBN-13: 978-0-87286-457-3
  ISBN-10: 0-87286-457-X
  I. Johnson, Rebecca.   II. Title.

  PJ7914.N88I3813 2007
  892.7'17—dc22

                                         2007005703

Visit our website: www.citylights.com

City Lights Books are published at the City Lights Bookstore, 261 Columbus Avenue, San Francisco, CA 94133.

Many thanks to Rebecca C. Johnson for her meticulous and hard work to allow *I`jaam* to speak another language.

For those who never returned!

"Write without any concern or hesitation that the government may or may not be satisfied with what you write."
— The Father-Leader

"As for writing, it protects man from oblivion. It transports the self to those who are distant and absent."

"To write is to risk being misread or misunderstood. Words that survive their author are cut loose. They drift, take new shape, sprout new meanings. And there is always their ordinary ambiguity"
— Ibn Khaldun, 14th-century historian

"Can you describe this?
"Yes," I said
And something like a smile
Passed through her face"
— Anna Akhmatova

A Note About *I`jaam*

The Arabic alphabet contains twenty-eight letters, half of which are pairs or triplets of letters with the same skeleton, but with variations of one, two, or three dots to represent different phonetic characters. Within each word, the letters are written differently depending on their position (beginning, middle, or end).

Initially, inscriptions and texts were written without dots, and the meaning could be deciphered from context and syntax. Later, to eliminate ambiguous readings of some letters, dots and diacritical marks were added to the Arabic script. Since the script was originally derived from Nabatean Aramaic, the "borrowing" of the dots from that script was termed *I`jaam (dotting)*, from the root `-j-m meaning "foreign/non-Arab/barbarous." Since this act of dotting had the effect of clarifying and elucidating, *I'jaam* also came to mean just that, i.e., "elucidating" and "clarifying."

In English, an uncrossed t might be misread as an l, but context and limited possibilities of sequences limit potential confusion. In Arabic, the richness of the root system and the high number of variations and combinations — since half of the letters have one, two, or three dots — produces a much more complex situation if one does not cross his or her t's. For example, undotted, the word *bayt* (house), could be dotted in a variety of ways to be read as *bint* (girl), *banat* (she built), *nabt* (plant), *thabt* (brave), and more. Context can help eliminate some of the possibilities, but there is still much space for ambiguity in an undotted manuscript, especially a handwritten one, such as that whose fate unfolds in this novel!

—Sinan Antoon

Introduction

Prison literature occupies a large space in the Arab literary scene nowadays, and it plays a dual role. On the one hand, it serves as a document of our reality, one that is besieged by dictatorships that crush humans. On the other, it is a laboratory for new literary styles, and a testimony to art's capacity to transform the resistance to death into a defense of life's powerful forces of self-renewal.

Resisting oppression through novels and poetry has become a cultural standard in post-colonial Arabic literature, and prison literature is one of its basic features. From Syria to Iraq, Palestine, Lebanon, Egypt and the Arab Maghreb, prison literature has moved from the margins to become the main text, because prison itself is not a margin, but rather the dominant sociopolitical experience. Our poets and novelists have occupied a form which allows them to use the prism of prison experience to expose the massive human suffering of the Arab whose citizenship has been confiscated and who has been deprived of his/her right to liberty. Sinan Antoon's *I`jaam* now joins this lineage, occupying a context created by the works of Sun`allah Ibrahim, Abdilrahman Munif, Fadhil al-`Azzawi, Faraj Bayraqdar and others.

I`jaam shares two basic features with most prison literature: muddled memory and writing as resistance. The prisoner conjures the past and all that exists beyond the prison's walls in order to create hope. But the past cannot be invoked except in a disjointed context, and it is in this way that prison literature reveals the extent to which contemporary life in the Arab world is itself disjointed and without logic. Entire countries have been turned into prisons, with the Arab "patriarch" in his perpetual autumn dominating all aspects of everyday life, turning the media and all public space into a mirror to idolize and mummify the present.

The prisoner resists by recording his experience in its immediacy; it's as if the soul stripped naked by barbaric torture can only be covered with words. He writes in his journal, or dreams of writing, or lives on in order to write, certain that he will triumph over his experience by writing it. A literature which renews literature is born, a writing that triumphs over oppression with dreams of liberty.

I`jaam is a novel about writing, and the writing here has two sources: memory and nightmare, and the distance between the two is so fragile that they often mix. The world of memories confronts the reality of prison, and the war is waged inside the prisoner. This is where the novel's game originates; memory takes us to life and the prison experience throws us into death. At their intersection comes writing, so that the story may escape beyond the walls.

In this beautiful and brilliant novel, Sinan Antoon expresses the voice of those whose voices were robbed by oppression, stressing the fact that literature can at times be the only framework to protect human experience from falling into oblivion. *I'jaam* is an honest and exciting window onto Iraq, written with both profound love and bitter sarcasm, hope and despair. It not only illuminates reality in Iraq prior to the American invasion, but also the shared human insistence on resisting oppression and injustice.

—Elias Khoury

I`jaam

an iraqi rhapsody

CLASSIFIED

Ministry of the Interior
Directorate of General Security
Baghdad District
8241976/G
22 August, 1989

To Whom It May Concern:

The enclosed manuscript was found in a
file cabinet during a general inventory,
taken in preparation for the move to
the new complex in al-Baladiyyat. The
manuscript appears to be handwritten and
without dots. A qualified personnel is
hereby requested to add the dots and
write a brief report of the manuscript's
contents to be submitted to our department by the end of this month.

Signature

J.S.A.

cc/archives

---

*Received 8/23/1989
 T.A. designated to carry out the task.

Two clouds kissed silently in the Baghdad sky. I watched them flee westward, perhaps out of shyness, leaving me alone on the bench beneath the French palm tree (so called because it stood in the courtyard in front of the French department) to wait for Areej. I looked for something worth reading in that morning's *al-Jumhuriyya*, and found a good translation of a Neruda poem in the culture section, besieged* on all sides by doggerel barking praises of the Party and the Revolution. The breeze nudged the palm fronds above my head to applaud. It was April, "the month of fecundity, the birth of the Ba`th and the Leader," as one of the posters on the college walls announced.

"Good morning."

I longed to hear the warm, milky voice of Areej, but this was not hers. It was the voice of Abu `Umar, the security officer enrolled as a student in the English department. He wore gray pants and an open-collared shirt. Accompanying him was another of his feces†—short, long-faced, with a thick mustache. This one wore a blue safari suit, the fashion of choice for all *mukhabarat*, the secret police, regardless of season or occasion.

"Comrade Salah," said Abu `Umar, introducing the short man, elongating the final "a" of his Samarra'i accent to make it sound closer to its Tikriti variation. Abu `Umar's reddish mustache reminded me of the cock-

---

*Beside?
† Species?

roaches that invaded our bathroom at night, thwarting our every eradication campaign. Like most of his colleagues, Abu `Umar never made any effort to conceal his occupation. He rarely attended classes, and his age (he was in his late thirties) was a clear sign that he wasn't an ordinary college student. In times of war, graduates were immediately conscripted, and except for graduate students who had secured special permission to continue their studies, no one could linger in college to change disciplines or get a second degree. Abu `Umar, however, transferred to the English department halfway through the academic year, after he had spent three years in the Arabic department.

"Comrade Salah would like to ask you a few questions," he said. I couldn't hide my anxiety, but I answered with an unhesitant, "Of course." Salah smiled viciously and asked me to come with him.

"Where?"

"To the office. It won't take more than half an hour."

I had thought a great deal about this moment, but could never seem to summon discretion enough to avoid it. Abu `Umar gathered the books stacked on the bench beside me and put them in my hands. We walked toward the main gate. I had always complained about the distance between the gate and the lecture halls, but that morning as we crossed the nearly empty courtyard the walk seemed mercilessly short. It was early still—I liked to arrive before most students to avoid Baghdad's morning crowds and traffic. I looked around for a familiar face, perhaps someone to record my absence, but found none. I thought of Areej and her incessant murmurs of caution. I thought of my grandmother with her endless praying and the candles she lit in church after church for my safety.

We crossed the courtyard that separated the English department from the dean's offices, passed by the Student Union, and turned left toward the main entrance. Through the iron gate I could see a Mitsubishi with tinted windows. It was parked beneath the mural erected in honor of the Leader's honorary doctorate in disorder.* He wore a university gown and held a degree in his hand. The inscription read, "The pen and the gun have one barrel."[†]

The Ministry of Rupture and Inflammation[‡] would daily bombard us with slogans and chants, and I retained my sanity by rearranging their words and images to better suit my mood. I began with some political songs, which could be improved with a simple stroke. In the name of the People and the Nation, I unsheathed my invisible pen and began to improve my superior's verses:

House by house
Our leader calls on us
And fucks[§] us into bed . . .

When we reached the car a man emerged from the driver's side and opened the back door. Salah motioned for me to get in. I gave Abu `Umar a contemptuous look

---

*Law?

[†] A saying of our great Leader, may God preserve him.

[‡] Could this be the Ministry of Culture and Information?

[§] The original lyrics read, "tucks."

and climbed onto the seat. It was clear that he would not be coming with us. Salah slammed the door shut and sat down next to me, while another man, bald with sunglasses, sat beside the driver.

The car left the college in the direction of al-Waziriyya. We passed a bookstore where I sometimes shopped, turned right at the Muhammad al-Qasim expressway, and south toward the People's Stadium. On the radio, the announcer read the morning news. A drop of sweat fell from my forehead onto the right lens of my glasses, mocking my attempt at composure. It was the first time I had felt real fear since the first days of the war, when Iranian jets thundered above Baghdad and dropped their bombs by the hundreds. The expressway ran over an old cemetery where it is said the grave of Zubayda, wife of Harun al-Rashid, lies—or perhaps another Zubayda of more recent demise. The image of the Syrian actress who played Zubayda in the television series about Harun al-Rashid imposed itself on my mind, along with the lyrics of Nazim al-Ghazali, also buried in that cemetery: "Those who threw me / those that tortured me / on a distant bridge have left me." What lies ahead for me? Sarmad was right to warn me. Did someone write a report? Did they hear me doing my impression of Him? My grandmother was right.

Please be careful, my son. For my sake. What would I do if anything happened to you? I'd die. They'll cut out your tongue. These people don't fear God. They fear nothing . . .

Salah interrupted her to answer my questions. Could he hear her, too?

"We have very much enjoyed your ideas. We'd like to hear more of them," he said with evident sarcasm. Glancing down at the cemetery as we quickly left it behind, he added, "and your famous sense of humor."

"What do you mean?"

"You know very well what I mean. We, too, know things, you see," he smiled.

The car left the expressway at al-Nidal Street. I knew we were heading toward General Security. The drops of sweat began to multiply on my forehead and my heart beat with a tribe of drums running one after another. The car crossed through the empty streets of the quiet neighborhood that surrounded the security complex. We passed a young girl riding a bicycle near the Iraqi National Symphony, which I knew was close to the security complex. (I used to joke about this harmonious coincidence of Baghdad's geography.) We passed the Ta`aruf Club, owned by the Sabean minority. I would go there sometimes with one of my Sabean friends to drink beer on their terrace. The car slowed to let the girl complete her turn, and I could see her mother outside of their door, screaming and waving her arms. Salah motioned for the driver to enter through "Gate Three." After a few minutes we stopped at a tall entrance guarded by three armed men. When they recognized the car they removed that iron shark's jaw that lies in front of every government building. As the gate opened the driver and the guards exchanged greetings, and the car began to move again.

Inside, Salah asked the driver to stop and open the trunk. The long street stretching in front of us was flanked on the left by a high wall topped with barbed wire and cameras. Salah got out of the car. I heard the sound of the trunk latching shut. He returned with a white cloth in his hands, and began to put it over my eyes. I reached out to resist, but he forced my hands down. "If you move again, I swear to God I'll crush your teeth."

I heard the scraping of the gate as it closed behind us. The last thing I saw was the Leader's face staring at me from Salah's Swiss watch. I reached up again to stop him, and felt a fierce blow at the back of my head. I don't remember what happened afterward.

I had returned to find my grandmother in front of the television, tea tray on the table. She was crying.

"What's wrong?" I asked.

"Come and see. A man from the Ministry of Interior was on the television and he said that citizens must start donating their eyes to support the war effort. He said they're using the schools as collection centers . . . They asked for money and we gave. They asked for gold and we gave. But this is just too much. May God send them all to hell! What times are we living in?"

I thought that senility had finally infiltrated her brain,

but the television announcer began to repeat the ministry's statement:

"Our great people! In your heroic battles with the Enemy you have watered the soil of this country with your precious blood. Our noble women have donated their gold to preserve our economy in its hour of need. And now our beloved nation appeals to you again to demonstrate to the Enemy your legendary bravery and boundless willingness to sacrifice . . ."

How could I have forgotten the absurd carnival our lives had become during these last years? Everything had become possible. I collapsed onto the couch beside my grandmother and picked up one of the day's newspapers. The letters of the headlines had no dots. I turned the pages and looked at the photographs. A terror struck me. The faces were eyeless. I leapt from the couch toward the door, with my grandmother's screamed warnings to "stay inside" running after me into the street.

Outside, the street signs, advertisements, and even license plates were without dots. I saw a line forming outside the middle school on our street—it had quickly been turned into an "Eye Donation Center." People were laughing and cheering, and some were even singing, "Everything you touched, our eyes kissed, the day you came, Oh great Leader . . ." The laughter and ululation grew louder. A man I didn't recognize pulled me into line. Party members in khaki uniforms recorded people's ages and eye color. I saw ʿAli, a friend from high school, standing near the end of one of the lines. Unlike the others, he was frowning. I wanted to ask him what was happening. I called his name, but he didn't hear me. The sound of the applause rose mercilessly.

I awoke to find myself (t)here.

Papers were scattered in front of me. `Ali! Where are you? Did you visit me in my nightmare to encourage me to write? You used to give me your journal to read, and I would labor to decipher your undotted script. To write or not to write? "Write without any concern or hesitation that the government may or may not be satisfied with what you write."* What could happen? They'll think that I have gone mad. And even if they find the papers, they won't be able to read them. My high school Arabic teacher used to complain that my handwriting looked like crab marks on sand.

I will wait.

I was sitting on my favorite bench beneath the French palm tree reading a newspaper when hesitating footsteps approached me. I looked up. It was a young man with a cigarette in his hand.

"Excuse me. Can I have a word with you?"

I knew that his name was Sarmad, and that we were

---

*His Excellency's saying from his famous speech to the Union of Writers and Journalists.

in the same year. We shared a taxi to a soccer match once, and we argued the whole way. He was a Tayaran fan. We exchanged greetings every now and then. He spoke in a low voice:

"I know we don't know each other, but think of me as a brother. I have only one thing to say—you'd better watch out, because they're after you. They say you're arrogant and have a big mouth. They're looking for something, anything, against you and you'll be gone. So please, be careful."

I asked him who he meant by "they," but he didn't answer. I remembered I had seen him before with "comrade" Ayad from the student government.

"Please, keep this between us," he added.

"But why should you care?"

"God forgive you!" he hissed. "Some of us still have a conscience!"

"Sorry, it's just a bit unusual."

"Just consider it an act of charity. I have to go. Good luck, and please take care."

Sarmad roused me from my recklessness. I decided from that day to be more careful. What good would my disappearance into their labyrinth do? That night, when I told my grandmother about the incident she doubled her usual dose of panicked warnings:

"Didn't I tell you to watch out? These people don't even fear God. Why meddle in politics, my son? What will you get except trouble? You know I'd die if you were hurt in any way. Isn't it enough that I lost your father and mother—you want to abandon me too? They'll cut out your tongue. And what will you get? God and the Virgin Mary protect you. I light candles in church every day for you, but you never listen."

"Don't worry, Grandma. Nothing will happen."

"Don't worry? How can I not worry? Don't you remember the story about the child who told a joke he'd heard at home, and how his kindergarten teacher wrote a report and had the child's father put in prison? That was in kindergarten. Just imagine how many like her they have in colleges. When will you come to your senses? And why are you so upset at the government, anyway? You don't even have to serve in the army. You're better off than all those men who have to fight and die in the war."

I reminded her that my exemption from military service was due to a benign tumor in the right side of my brain, and not the beneficence of the government. But she continued to chastise me until I promised her I would be more careful. I promised myself I would try.

I woke up to find myself (t)here.

Baghdad's July is sadistic. The sun's rays lash the backs of its inhabitants, burning into their pores to roil every cell. Perhaps this is why all of our "revolutions" choose

July as their month to demonstrate their accomplishments. We have been taught to call these frequent events "revolutions," when they are actually scars on our history. A bunch of sadists get sunstroke and declare themselves saviors. Then they begin to torture people and ride them like mules, especially after they discover that this is easier, and perhaps more pleasurable, than fulfilling their promises. Later, another group will come along to depose the first, bringing with them longer whips and chains of a more economic metal. A sadistic circle forever strangling us. A political scientist would probably have little trouble disproving my theory, but in this heat and misery it appears, at least to me, a sound one.

To live here means to piss away* three quarters of your life waiting. Waiting for things that rarely come: Revolution, the bus, a lover, Godot . . . and waiting so long that you drown in time, because time itself is a fugitive citizen, trembling with fear and stumbling on the sidewalk, only to be pissed and spat upon by a merciless History. I felt a cool breeze when I remembered that Falah would be on his way. Or perhaps diabetes was no longer considered sufficient grounds for exemption from military service. We were comrades in illness and soccer mania, and shared a love for the arts. Falah was a talented painter, but his work suffered from one inexorable fault that prevented him from staging an exhibit: he refused to include a portrait of the Leader in his portfolio. Even established painters, who could afford to

---

*Pass?

ignore this unspoken rule, were called on from time to time to express their gratitude in newspaper or television interviews for the limitless support given to Iraqi fine arts by the Ultimate Artist.

It was our third day at the Ministry of Defense's "Special Committee" for reexamination. The experts and military physicians on this committee, handpicked by the Leader himself, were to subject all those previously exempted from military service to renewed scrutiny. It was said that those exempted for reason of obesity would be filmed to allow Him himself to render the final decision. And there would be no exemptions made this time for those citizens with "connections," who had previously been declared unfit even though they were as healthy as racehorses. Much was made of the unwavering justice of this new committee, but I still could not imagine relatives of important officials fighting on the frontlines, even if they were found to be fit. They would most likely be assigned to an administrative unit in their hometown and struggle to show up once a month in order to avoid embarrassing their commanding officer.

The first two days, we waited for hours only to be rewarded with the most common sentence in bureaucratic parlance: come back tomorrow. It reminded me of a cartoon I had clipped from *Alif Ba'* magazine and hung on my bedroom wall (as well as the wall of my memory): a government employee sits behind a desk like an emperor, and in front of him stands a poor citizen,

fatigued after a long day in search of signatures and
stamps. The citizen, out of breath and dripping sweat,
needs just one more signature to finish his task, but the
bureaucrat tells him, "Come back tomorrow so I can tell
you to come back tomorrow."

I sought shelter from the tyranny of the sun in the
slender shade of a palm tree standing across the street
from the Ministry building. The sun, it seemed, had
allied itself with the status quo against us and beat down
its midday heat. Why had the Ministry of Defense
chosen this quiet residential neighborhood for its offices?
It was a dismal scene. Flocks of men lined up to enter
the building, some leaning on a cane and others on a
daughter, or son, or wife. Most of them carried envelopes,
mostly likely concealing X-rays or medical records,
despite the fact that we had been instructed not to bring
such documentation. The committee had decided that it
would recognize no previous diagnosis and would
instead rely solely on its own "evidence." Quick-thinking
entrepreneurs had availed themselves of this opportunity
and began to sell sandwiches and soft drinks to those
standing in line. After only a few minutes (we said we
would keep our appointment on "English time"), Falah
appeared across the street. I said goodbye to the gentle
tree and walked toward him.

We entered the gate and turned right, stopping in front
of a soldier who was preparing to read a list of names.
There was a group of about fifty men waiting—standing,

as they offered no benches or chairs, despite the fact that we were all considered "damaged" in some way. Perhaps keeping us standing under the burning sun was a new treatment developed by the Ministry of Defense? Falah and I squatted against a wall.

The soldier stood at the top of a concrete staircase leading to the entrance of the building. He read his list in a steady monotone. When we heard our names, we were to call out "yes" or "here" or "present"—anything to prove our existence at that particular moment. Falah found a pebble on the ground and began to draw something in the dust between his feet. A man in his forties approached me, wearing the thickest glasses I had ever seen, and asked the time. It was almost noon.

"A watch is an instrument for measuring lost time," I said to Falah, as if I had just made a discovery that would benefit mankind.

"That's a good first line for a story," he said.

As one name followed another, some of the men began to chat; others asked the soldier to reread a name. The rising babble no doubt offended the sensitive ears of the soldier, as he stopped reading the names and stared at us long enough to silence the entire crowd. Then a lecture began in a thick Tikriti accent:

"Look, I'm sick of this shit. You're not children. If you hear your name, say 'yes.' And stand in line. This isn't a coffeehouse or a Turkish bath. I don't want hear any bullshit. Get it? Or are you too deaf and stupid to understand? Look, those who do get it can explain it to the others. I'm going to read these names and if I hear any of you say one word I'll stamp your military service booklet right now and have you transferred to the front-lines within forty-eight hours. My commanding officer will be more than happy to get rid of you sick bastards. And if you want to complain, go ahead. My name is Hasan; I dare you to file a complaint."

He sighed and went back to his list, trying to find the last name he had read. I looked at Falah, who smiled sarcastically and nodded his head silently. The man in the thick glasses mumbled something I couldn't make out. The frustration of the crowd was visible in their tired eyes. But who would say anything? Falah's name was called, and he stood.

"Wait for me?"

"Yeah, I'll be in front."

"*Zayn*. See you soon."

He joined the others in a long line. The officer called three more names before he led the group into the building. After a few minutes more he came back out and began reading names from a new sheet. My name was on the third list. I stood in the line and entered the door.

When I was eighteen, I reported for my first examination at the military conscription center. At the time, it was carried out by one military physician and took only ten minutes. Now it's different. The soldier ordered us to remove our clothes to our undergarments, divided us into groups of five, and directed us to sit on the benches that lined the long hallway leading to the examination room. We were to enter the examination room, stand silently in front of the committee, and speak only when asked a question. A soldier stood on either side of the hallway, and a third at the door to the room. I took off my clothes and spent about ten minutes sitting on the bench, enjoying the cool streams that flowed from the committee's air conditioners. I began to contemplate the possibility of conscription, but before I could fully rehearse the anxiety that followed that thought, I heard my name called. I walked toward the room, and the soldier at the door told me to stop. I watched another young man leave the room, and heard the order to enter. Three men in white coats sat behind a wide table, and the Leader observed the proceedings from a photo above their heads. Below his portrait read an inscription written in angular, Kufic script: "The sweat shed in training lessens the blood shed in battle."* Another man stood in the middle of the room to my left. He looked younger than the other three, who were probably all in their fifties. After they had read the forms in front of them, one asked me to extend my arms. My right arm appeared normal and strong, while my left, weak because of a benign tumor that was found in my brain when I was twelve, drooped like a withering branch.

"Walk forward a little," said the one in the middle. I hoped they would notice my slight limp, which was

---

*A saying of our venerable Leader, may God preserve him.

more pronounced that day because of the whisky Falah and I had drunk the night before. I had walked to within a meter of the table when he stopped me and said, "Enough. Turn and walk back to where you were standing." They each began to write on their papers and the one in the middle told me to leave.

"And the verdict?" I asked.

"It will appear on your military service booklet at your conscription center."

I left the room and dressed quickly. The soldier at the door pointed the way out. I breathed a sigh of relief, despite the disappointment of the postponed decision. Falah was waiting outside. They had asked him about his daily insulin injections and demanded to see their marks. We visited the conscription center in eastern Karada four times during the following month before we received the results; we had been declared "unfit for military service." The committee, it seems, had introduced new vocabulary — before, we were considered "exempt." Damaged goods in times of war.

These words recorded in our booklets didn't quite overwhelm us with joy, but it did spread a tranquil comfort over us to know that our death might be postponed until the next committee, or the next war. We celebrated by going to *Mansur Mansur*, our favorite bar. It was on Sadoun Street, next to the Iranian Airlines office that had been vandalized during the first days of the war in 1980; it was burned and now served as an impromptu toilet for drunken passersby. We drank a toast to disability and listened to Umm Kulthum sing "Forgetfulness is Bliss." That day we sat next to an old man—a permanent fixture in the bar. According to the waiter, he came in every day at three and sat alone at the corner table with his only son's photograph in front of him. The son had been missing in action for four years. The old man would sit and drink, bottles crowding around the photograph, while he wailed and called out his son's name: Salam . . . Salam . . .

I went home. My grandmother had prepared the tea for our regular afternoon chat. She began to narrate the events of her day:

"You should have seen what happened in church today. They brought in the body of this young man, a soldier, so handsome. Like the moon! And his father had gone mad, just mad. He was dancing and singing, 'My son's not dead. He's not dead.' Poor thing. He was an engineer and left two children behind. His wife was there, too. She was tearing out her hair. How they cried! And his father danced and cried like a woman."

I asked her about this sudden change in religious atmosphere: "Since when do they play music in church?"

"Not inside! They were outside, next to the door. Whenever they bring in a soldier a group of those Party members come and play music. Why don't you come to church once in while if you want to know what goes on there? One like you, no religion . . ."

I evaded the rest of that lecture by asking another question. "What music did they play?"

"I don't know. It was . . . 'The Land Is Your Mother'. That's it."

Khalid had once convinced me to submit some of my stories to *Jumhuriyya*, and he even offered to take them himself to the editor of the cultural review, whom he happened to know at the time. I wasn't very hopeful—most of what they published were stories by authors like themselves, who wrote celebratory prose in the meter, beat out by the war drum. But Khalid insisted, and I agreed. I gave him a story about the delirium of a grief-stricken mother who waits for the body of her only son to return from the war. The editor rejected it, of course, on the grounds that it was not useful for "mobilization purposes." The mother of a martyr should be proud and greet the body of her martyred son with songs of joy, he told me. For were not "the martyrs nobler than us all"?*

I dig in this silence, searching for a yet deeper silence to burrow into, but the screaming assaults me again. I smear the walls with my insanity, as if to ward off the screams that creep nearer and nearer. Screams mingled with a mocking laughter. I am laughing too, and then I cry. I see a tall door in front of me stretching from the floor to the ceiling. I reach to open it. A long path

---

*A saying of our great Leader (may God preserve him).

appears, lined with trees in whose thick branches rustle all the letters of the alphabet. As I step onto the path, a storm wind blows. I hear a murmuring in the branches—the dots of the letters are falling from the trees like autumn leaves, and the letters are left as bare as branches. The letters fall too, each pronouncing its own sound as it strikes the ground. The wind calms, and silence once again unfolds itself. The letters are changing color, from black to dark green, to light green. They begin to stir, spinning in spirals on the path. They are grasshoppers, turning and jumping. They spring into the trees. They are locusts. They bite hungrily into the branches. They swallow trees whole. The wind howls again, pushing me back inside. The door closes and fades away, but I can still hear the locusts ruining the silence.

"Democrassy is a source of strength for the individual and society,"* read the signs the day of the student council elections that year. One of the comrades interrupted our English literature lecture to ask our professor, who was busy describing the major trends of modern literary criticism, to end the class early so that we could participate in this simulation† of Democracy. There had been no campaigning or debates, nor any other method of discerning one candidate's platform from another's; not that it was necessary—they were all Ba`thists and members of the Student Union. The entire process

---

*Democracy? One of the Father-Leader's sayings.
† Celebration?

amounted to the observation of a single table, on which were placed name cards, and behind which the candidates sat silently. The year before I had voted for Mickey Mouse — they don't read what we write on those slips of paper anyway. But that year we decided to vote for different people. I chose one with the same first name as my favorite soccer player, and you voted for the most handsome one. I remember feeling jealous, and your smile when you said, "He won't win."

I feel an intense pain in the back of my head from the blow I received when I tried to resist. It becomes aggravated when he pulls my hair or pushes my head, rubbing my nose in that gray cloth that has been colonized by a foul smell — a mixture of sweat, blood, and layers of dirt. The pain surges to my wrists and joints when I try to pry open the wires that cut into my skin. I can feel his sticky fingers on my right thigh as he holds me down. His dirty fingernails dig into my skin. I close my eyes and try to disappear from existence, to flee my body, to abandon it forever . . . ah, if only I could shed it, exchange it for another form. It's no use. I don't remember his face. Perhaps I'm trying to forget it. But I can't ever forget his voice, whispering in my ear while his whole weight lay like a corpse on top of me:

"You know you're my favorite. With the others it's work, but with you it's pleasure. You're much tighter than the others; it must be your first time. What an ass you have! Why don't you clap? You faggot! I'll make your ass clap."

My hands were tied in the position of eternal applause. His hot breath burned my neck and inflamed my disgust. He would talk and laugh at first, but he'd soon give over to a soft panting as he was about to ejaculate. Then I would hear the zipper, followed by a slap on my ass, and the "thanks" that marked the end of the ritual. Many small things shattered inside of me every time, things I can't name or identify. But their shards still wound me. When I stopped crying aloud and left the screams to echo inside my own depths, he would say, "Why aren't you whining any more? Started to enjoy it?"

He called himself Abu Khalid. I learned this from his colleague, who helped to restrain me — he'd stand outside until Abu Khalid signaled that he was finished with me. He would politely thank him when Abu Khalid invited him to "have a taste," but always declined.

Perhaps they have won, with all this filth they've smeared on the walls of my memory and subconscious — their slogans that reek of piss, the shit that piles up in the abandoned streets of my body. How can I be rid of it without dying myself, or going mad? Their chants penetrate my ears and eyes and seep out of my anus, only to invade again through my mouth, and I have no choice but to swallow them, while they mock me.

We heard in the morning that there would be a demonstration in support of the Leader. The Enemy had called for referendums in both countries to show the popularity of the two regimes, suggesting that whichever Leader showed the least popular support should step down and accept defeat, thus ending the war without further bloodshed. The Party mobilized all its branches to organize the public's "spontaneous" demonstration of their love for the Leader. And so the comrades came, arriving halfway through first period to ask us to assemble in the main yard and listen to speeches before we joined the larger demonstration outside the school grounds. They warned us that anyone caught trying to leave the assembly would be severely punished and expelled from school.

In those days we saw demonstrations as an opportunity to escape our boring classes and to try to talk with the girls from neighboring schools. We were all assembled in the main yard, with each teacher standing at the front of his or her class. We formed a rectangle, with the flag undulating high above its heart. The head principal, his assistants, and members of the Student Union stood in front of the main building, overlooking the yard. The head principal, Professor Qutayba, delivered a passionate oratory urging us to show our gratitude to our historic leadership. We were, after all, its future soldiers. Our voices should shake the world, he said. Then he asked us to repeat after him, "Yes, yes to our Leader. Yes, yes to our Leader." We shouted for five minutes and then applauded. The head of the Student Union followed with a short speech. He told us that today "was the day to renew our pledge of allegiance to our Leader-Father." Then came time for poetry, and one of our young poetic masters recited his "Pledge of Blood," in which he proclaimed our loyalty to the Party and our willingness to die for the Leader and the homeland. Then the head principal instructed us all to join the other schools. We took the flags and placards distributed by the comrades from the Union of Iraqi Students. We reached the main street in al-A'zamiyya and headed towards Bab al-Mu'azzam where the masses were to converge. All the sidestreets were heavily guarded to make sure no one would sneak out. It was futile anyway, since it was impossible to find a bus or a cab on days such as this one. Most of Baghdad would come to a standstill; all the main roads were blocked and we would have to walk back home on foot. We spent more than an hour on our way to Bab al-Mu'azzam. The comrades would at times urge us to chant zealously, but our chants would die out when the comrade tended to another part of the demonstration. The organizers had tried this time to segregate the girls and boys as much as possible, but once we approached Bab al-Mu'azzam chaos reigned. We escaped the comrades' censorship and went on the prowl for girls. There were thousands of heads under the Leader's pictures, and placards indicating the school or

Party branch. The expansion of the Madinat al-Tibb
hospital was underway in the northern part of Bab
al-Mu'azzam, and the foreign company in charge of the
project, or perhaps the resident engineer, contributed to
the ritual as well. A huge crane lifted a gigantic picture
of the Leader high above and moved it left to right, like
a giant totem amidst an ocean of applause and cries of
"Yes, yes to our Leader."

Her slender body caught my eye right away. She was
wearing a blue skirt that barely covered her knees and a
white shirt light enough to reveal the pear-like breasts
imprisoned in her black bra. She was perhaps sixteen—
olive-skinned, with hazel eyes, short black hair and a
seductive smile. She played with her hair, announcing to
the world her discomfort in the heat and the crowds.
Encouraged by the looks we exchanged, I tried to move
closer, weathering many complaints and curses, especially from the more conservative girls: "Where in God's
name are you going?" I lied and told them I was looking
for my cousin. When I finally reached her, I was able to
position myself behind her. Another wave carried us
both forward, and I was pushed against her. My head
almost hit hers. I could smell her hair and feel her supple
ass against me before I retreated a step. She turned
around and exclaimed in exaggerated, and very seductive, alarm:

"Ayy . . . what's going on?"

"Sorry. I got a push from behind."

She smiled and turned forward again. Her full lips pouted a bit, and I noticed that the lower one was a bit bigger than the upper. Their redness awakened the desire that occupied my adolescent body. I was dying to taste the smoothness of her neck, out of which jutted a tiny mole on the left side. She stroked her hair again and turned back to flash me an encouraging smile. The roar of thousands of small volcanoes filled my blood, pressing me forward once again. I felt a hard-on so strong it threatened to pierce my pants. I though she might turn around and slap me, and that everyone around her would join in—like the time when a student from our school stood behind a girl getting on the bus. But I kept pushing gently every now and then. I pretended it was the motion of the crashing waves. Yes, Yes to our Leader. Yes, Yes. She didn't react, at first. But then I felt her pushing her body backward. Yes, Yes. Our mutual rhythm started slowly and then hastened, gaining its own momentum. I looked behind us to see if anyone had noticed our sinful dance. The surging waves hid us. Yes, Yes to our Leader. This was the first and last time a political chant expressed my true desires. A delicious pudendum* of a different sort. I could, for a moment, forget the Leader and scream: Yes, Yes.

> I woke up to find myself still (t)here,
> soaked in a sticky warmth.

---

*Referendum?

They allowed me to shower. I thought that they might be moving me to another prison or bringing me to trial. Did they find what I had written? Had Ahmad betrayed me? Was it all a trick? I asked the fat one what the occasion was. He laughed, "It's your wedding night. We're grooming you. But first we have to circumcise you." He laughed again. I was, in fact, circumcised, but he was referring to the mistaken belief that Christians in our country don't circumcise their children.

"Can you get it up, or have you forgotten how?"

The other one liked to feminize me: "Come on. Time to clean up, bitch." I took my time under the warm water and breathed the scent of olives in the soap. It was my favorite brand, Ghar al-'Isa, which made me question the reality of my situation. I thought I would wake up from the long nightmare, but I didn't. They led me down a cold, narrow corridor, and then Fatso pushed me into a room to the right. A man sitting behind the desk told Fatso he'd call for him when he was finished. Fatso left and shut the door behind him.

"Please, have a seat."

He pointed to a metal chair in front of his desk. I sat down slowly. It was the first time I had sat on a chair in ages. I felt pain in my anus and lower back. So, the shower was for the benefit of this man . . .

"What would you like to drink?"

I was shocked by the tenderness of his tone, and didn't know what to reply. Had they suddenly decided to respect international conventions for the protection of human rights? He added, as though he had noticed this thought run through my mind, "We do know how to be hospitable." He laughed. I remained silent. After a few seconds an old man knocked and entered.

"Yes, sir?"

"Two cups of tea, please."

My host was in his late thirties. He had short black hair, brown eyes, and a thick mustache in the style of the "Eighth of February" revulsion.* He wore a white shirt open at the collar. A gray jacket hung in the corner of the room, and a black umbrella leaned on the white wall below it. Drops of water slowly slid down it and fell to the ground like tears. So, it's raining? I couldn't hear it from in my cell. Oh, those walls! Nothing but walls. I tried to remember clouds, but the sound of his voice frightened them away.

"Do you smoke?"

"No, thank you," I replied calmly.

"That's wise. Quite right."

What was the point of this show? I had never seen this "sir" before, nor heard his voice. He took a cigarette from a pack of Sumer (apparently he supports national industries), and then replaced the pack on the table next to a clock with golden arms and a portrait of the Leader in military dress as its face. "Greetings from the Ministry of the Interior," read the caption below it. The clock read 8:30. Papers and files lay scattered on the table. He

---

*Revolution?

moved his chair backward and exhaled. A cloud of smoke, on its way to the ceiling, crossed a metal-framed placard that read, "We are strong but not arrogant, modest but never weak."* To its left was another photo of the Leader with his youngest daughter. I remembered one of my favorite jokes: a depressed man goes to a psychiatric clinic for treatment and tells the doctor that he cannot stand living in this world, so the doctor prescribes him a drug that will allow him to sleep for fifty years and wake up when the world has changed. The depressed man is elated, buys the drug, sleeps, and wakes up fifty years later to find everything as it was, with the Leader's grandson in office and the crowds chanting for him.

There was a knock on the door, and the old man entered with two cups of tea. I had the inexplicable feeling that the "sir" knew I had thought of that joke. I had not yet learned my lesson. How can I stop the spontaneous leap from words to images to meaning? Ha— here I am, practicing self-censorship! "We want the Iraqi's own conscience to be his censor!"† Yes. I looked for a calendar on the wall, but found no way of knowing where in time I was located. I noticed a diary next to an ashtray, but could not read the date. I had lost consciousness, and track of the days, several times since I had begun to keep count. I had once asked one of them what day it was and he laughed, "Why, have a date?"

"Please, drink."

---

*A saying of our illustrious Leader.

† A saying of our great Father-Leader (may God protect him).

His cigarette remained held tight between his fingers while he stirred his tea. I lifted my own hand to take a sip, and then returned the glass to the tray. Cardamom. It reminded me of those short hours of afternoon when my grandmother and I would chat in front of the television. Does she know that I'm here? Is she trying to find me? He took two sips of his tea, and then returned his cigarette to his lips.

"You are a poet?"

"I write," I said. He laughed.

"Such modesty." After a heavy silence he added, "I myself am a great admirer of poetry. I published an "ode" once in *al-Qadisiyya*. I wanted to chat, but perhaps I am too traditional for you and your colleagues. I write in monorhyme, like our great ancestors used to."

I wasn't prepared to get into the polemics of the prose poem and its legitimacy. I thought maybe he was bored, and wanted an audience for his idiotic opinions. Am I the fortunate listener? I was honest with him.

"There are some good monorhyme poems," I told him. He laughed.

"No need for pleasantries. You know, I look at this subject from an ethical and political perspective, not just a literary one. Culture can never be divorced from reality. For example, we are, right now, in a state of war. Not only are our borders threatened, our very existence is threatened as well. Every creative act, then, must aid in mobilizing the people. You can't just write about the sea, or science fiction. Separating culture from reality is regressive, and treasonous. This modern poetry of yours, and especially the so-called 'prose poem,' is pure nonsense. How can you ignore fifteen hundred years of literary tradition and run after silly foreign fads? I say it's unethical. After everything that the party has done for this generation, to be so ungrateful . . . You, for example, you are a student. But, unlike in most countries, you pay no tuition. Even your books are provided by the Party. Everything is given to you. And how do you express your gratitude? With arrogance, with disdain for all we hold sacred."

I said nothing, of course. It was useless, anyway. The comrades always talk about responsibilities, but forget rights, those other sacred objects. I could hear faint music coming from a small radio. He opened one of the files sitting on his desk and leafed through its contents. I don't remember how long this meeting lasted, or anything he said after he turned the pages of the file. But I do remember that in the end he called for them to remove me, and that as I was being led out he said, "It's no use. You'll never be civilized."

I was waiting for Falah in front of the stadium. The match was to start in fifteen minutes, and I had already bought the tickets. The Tawari' Forces, usually protecting the Republican Palace, supervised the stadium's security on those occasions when the Leader's son was to attend. They arrived late that day, and their tardiness caused some disarray; long lines of spectators formed to enter the stadium. When Falah arrived, we joined the crowds, pushing and shoving our way to the entrance. We were searched (the first in a series of searches) and our tickets taken, but once inside there was yet another set of gates to pass through. Hundreds of soldiers, leading German shepherds, tried to organize our entry through the seven gates leading to the stadium. Most of them were not yet twenty but were, thanks to their brutal training, more rabid than the dogs they had on leash. They lacked the experience, and perhaps the intelligence, however, to successfully carry out their assignment. Some used their thick batons to beat those of us not standing in line, or any who had strayed to the left or right. In moments of above-average chaos, they would unleash the dogs to bite us, and laugh. Falah and I stood quietly in one of the lines. The gate in front of us was closed for no apparent reason. We heard loud cheers coming from inside and realized that the two teams were already out on the field. The soldier in charge of our line waved his baton and screamed in warning, "If you make a fucking move, I'll break this on your back. Stand in lines like humans, and you'll get in!"

A man in his fifties wearing a suit asked, politely, that the gate be opened so we didn't miss the first minutes of the game. The soldier shut him up with a curse. Another soldier was walking back and forth, using his baton to make sure the line was straight and touching us each on our shoulder with the baton as if counting a flock of sheep. We heard the referee's whistle announcing the start of the match. Many of us began to lose patience. The gate was finally opened, and because the soldiers were too slow in this third round of searching us, many ran straight to the gate. The soldiers began to strike anyone within reach. One screamed, "You'll never be civilized! Never!"

I lost my wallet after that game. Al-Zawra had flooded al-Rashid's nets with three goals, and the al-Rashid players, on top of losing, were sentenced to three days' military detention. I lost some money that day, and also my university identification card. I was told to see the college security officer to request a new ID.

Comrade Abu Ahmad, wearing his blue safari suit as usual, told me that in cases of lost IDs, procedure requires a full investigation be made before a new card will be issued. I was surprised by the gravity of the situation, and when my surprise became apparent, Abu Ahmad grew annoyed. He said in a condescending tone, "You *are* aware that there are people who forge these identification cards and sell them to deserters?"

The number of army desertions had increased recently, as had the search parties and inspection points designed to recover them. Orders were announced to shoot deserting soldiers, even if they were not attempting to flee. Public executions, too, became commonplace, to be "a consideration for those who are considering desertion." Everyone in the district was requested to attend.

Abu Ahmad asked me to follow him into another room, where one of his assistants would take over. This assistant was the same comrade who stood in front of the college in the morning and forbade students who didn't adhere to the dress code, or didn't shave their beards, from entering the campus. He asked me to sit, took a white piece of paper from a drawer, and began speaking in classical Arabic. This move to the arena of official discourse appealed to me, so I answered him in a formal Arabic I was sure he wouldn't be able to follow.

"Can you inform as to where and when the identity card became lost?"

"I believe that it went missing during my attendance at a sporting event two days hence."

"Did you attempt to locate it?"

"Yes, I performed a full and thorough search of the area in question, to no avail." He shot me a look of annoyance after the "no avail" part.

"Are you not aware that the identity card stands as an important document, which one must protect?"

"Yes, I am. But it became lost or perhaps stolen—only God knows. But the reason for its absence is not neglect on my part."

"Do you swear to protect your new identity card from theft or harm, and to return your previous card if you are to find it?"

"Yes," I answered. He then returned to the colloquial to ask me to sign the "report."

"Go pay the fine in accounting, then bring me the receipt and two photos. You'll get the ID in a day or two."

When I arrived home my grandmother was watching television, as usual. The Leader was awarding a medal of courage to a man who killed his son for refusing to return to his military unit. When the "hero" was asked to narrate the details of his heroism, though, it appeared as though he had killed his son after an argument that had no relationship to nationalist duty, but rather a family dispute. It didn't matter. His heroism was used to embolden the spirit of victory and to establish the icon of a new citizen — one who puts country before all else, even his own blood. My grandmother clapped her hands together in disbelief.

"We live and see. What kind of animal is he? Doesn't he fear God?"

Here I am, carried away like a child who has discovered a new game. I must think. I am sure there is no camera. The building is old and not originally designed as a prison. It must have been an old house converted into a prison. I can hear footsteps approaching my door well before the guards appear, which gives me enough time to hide my papers under the mattress. But even if they were discovered, they would just think I had gone mad. But Ahmad? If he is telling the truth, he'll pay the price.

In March, my senior thesis advisor asked me to submit a topic for approval. I had read *Animal Farm* two months earlier, along with an article about *1984* that I had found in the college library. I thought I would write about *1984*, but Areej opposed the idea, warning that the paper would only cause me problems. "And it won't prove anything, anyway," as she said. But I was determined. I went to the library, found the title in the card catalogue, and took the card to Umm Sa`d, the librarian, who knew me well. She looked at the call number and walked to the shelves behind her, only to return empty-handed a few minutes later.

"Sorry, dear, I can't give you this book."

"Why?"

"It's banned."

I told her that I needed it for my thesis, but she insisted that she couldn't help me.

"It's not in my hands. A special committee decides these things. They just send us a list."

"Can I take it for just two hours, to photocopy it?" None of my appeals convinced her to break the rules, but as she closed those doors she opened another one.

"The only way is to get permission from the chair," she told me.

"*Zayn.* I'll go talk to him right now."

I had a good relationship with Dr. Khalid, the chair of the English department. He taught a class in drama my first year, and enjoyed a paper I wrote comparing Hamlet to the modern intellectual. I found him in front of his office talking with another professor. I waited until they had finished their conversation, and then greeted him and explained my situation. He smiled.

"Why do you want to get us into trouble, son?" He paused, and then corrected himself. "Not that it's anything dangerous, of course. It's about Stalinist regimes. I read it when I was at the University of Chicago. But, best to find another topic." He patted me on the shoulder, adding, "Take care of yourself, son."

I thanked him and left. I looked for a copy in the library of the British Council, just a short walk from the university. But I was told that it had been checked out, and was due almost a month ago. I talked to Professor Tariq, who is in charge of theses, and asked him for an extension without mentioning that the book was banned. He refused, though, and rejected the thesis topic in its entirety.

"Who is this Orwell?" he asked. "Never heard of him."

Professor Tariq, the feces advisor,* had received his Master's degree in English language and literature through a devotion to the Party, spending his graduate years spying on his colleagues and writing reports, rather than essays. He presented me with the brilliant alterna-

---

*Theses advisor?

tive topic of translating the Leader's speeches into English and studying them as literary texts. In the end, I decided to choose another topic and keep Orwell for a future thesis.

The moan of a door woke me, shattering a sleep that rarely takes shape before it is broken by a scream, or the sound of a door opening and closing. I could no longer make things out clearly. One of them stood over me and threw a pile of papers on my face.

"Go on, our young poet! Write! Maybe they'll give you the Nobel in prison, and Iraq can finally take some pride in you."

I didn't move. I had learned lessons here I could never comprehend outside. To be silent, to act slowly, deliberately. Is this another trick designed to humiliate me? Do they need evidence? For what?

I didn't move. I didn't touch the papers, or the pen lying next to them, even though I was sure there was no camera. Now I am no longer sure. Perhaps it was a nightmare. But I remember another. Yes, his face is clearer now. Mid-twenties, a thin, black mustache and black, penetrating eyes. He opened the door, closed it gently, and knelt close to me. He put some paper and a ballpoint pen by my feet.

"Hello," he whispered. "I asked them to transfer me when I heard there was a writer here. My father wrote novels. You've probably heard of him—Hassan al-Awqati—he died before the revolution. I'll try to bring you something to read. I'll be back, *zayn*?" He put his hand on my shoulder as he talked and looked behind. He said his name was Ahmad, and then he left.

There was a gleam of earnestness in his eyes. Could I be so lucky? Another outsider on this vast inside? But no—I can no longer trust my senses, or my intuition. It had been days, maybe weeks, since the last "party," as they called it ("Come on, you're the guest of honor"). Perhaps they were busy with others. I thought I had heard a new voice a few days ago.

I sat cross-legged in the corner of my cell, my head between my hands in a futile attempt to squeeze out the pain. The throbbing in my molar had migrated to inside my head and had begun to beat me mercilessly. When I asked for a doctor, they laughed. The fat one said, "Do you want us to get you a nurse, too? Where do you think you are, the Sheraton? Why don't you suck on my cock for a while? It's an old remedy I learned from your mother."

I'll wait. Maybe this is all just another nightmare. But if it's not, why would this Ahmad be risking so much for me? Perhaps he feels guilty for working with them. I knew a lot of people who have been forced to work in the system, and who still didn't lose their humanity. Is Ahmad, if that is really his name, one of them? I don't know.

I woke up to find myself (t)here.

Professor Kamal was discussing the rise of the theatre of the absurd when a knock on the classroom door interrupted him, and a comrade in a khaki suit entered. The time has come when one absurdity regularly interrupts another. A rumor had been circulating that morning that there would be a demonstration to celebrate the latest victory. Of course, at times like these, intellectual expressions must end in order for the revolution to continue.

"Pardon me, professor, but a demonstration will begin shortly. All are requested to gather in the main square."

The professor gathered his papers in silence. He didn't utter a word. How could he, a former socialist who had spent long years in a place like this? He came out broken, looking more like one of Beckett's characters than his former self.

A few moments later, the comrades from the Iraqi National Student Union were herding us to the square. Lecture halls and classrooms were locked. Some of us tried to stay behind by going to the cafeteria, but its manager had been instructed to turn out the customers and bolt the doors. Windows were latched. We filtered into the main square of the college, in front of a balcony holding a number of party officials and professors who would give speeches before the demonstration began.

Years before, another comrade named Nawfal had interrupted a geography lesson. We were in the middle of our first year of high school, and the war with Iran in its first months. The fashion for party members to wear khaki was in its infancy. Mrs. Hana', our geography teacher, was showing us on the map how the Euphrates passes through Syria and enters Iraq at al-Qa'im, when the comrade, in his military uniform, burst into the classroom. After a lecture about the free education given to us by the Party, he explained that the least we could do to show our gratitude was to become members. Some of us excused ourselves from the weekly meetings with homework or other activities, but comrade Nawfal countered all of our excuses with a simple gesture — passing out membership forms for us all to sign.

In addition to the ordinary information — name, religion, nationality — there were questions that many of us did not know how to answer: Do you have any distant relatives living outside of the country? But the most dangerous document that we, as thirteen-year-olds, had to sign was the pledge that we did not belong to any "enemy" parties (the al-Da`wa party, or the Communist party, among others). Not admitting this meant we would face the death sentence. The irony was that declaring membership in any of these parties would lead to the same sentence anyway. The next Monday after classes, we went to the first meeting. The leader, a fourth-year student, explained the structure of the Party, and our roles in it as its untiring eyes, "that watch for enemies wherever they might be—whether at home, in the street, or at school—and never miss an opportunity to report a suspicious activity or person." I noticed early on the essential contradictions in his speech. If all people loved the Party and the Revolution, how could it have enemies? He passed out the official report of the Eighth Regional Conference and asked us to read the first section for next week's meeting. The comrade in charge taught us the rules for writing reports. Party slogan on the right, followed by group, division, branch, and organization.

When I got home, I began to look over the book, and found that the last chapter was devoted to Party positions on current issues. In the section about Palestinian issues there was an attack on a king described as "the agent." Yet this king had visited Iraq more than once in the previous months to express his support for Iraq in the war, and on television his name was always preceded by "his majesty . . . sovereign of the kingdom . . ." In our second meeting, I asked the comrade about this, and he answered hesitatingly that this was an old report, and that they would distribute a revised one by next week. He then reprimanded me for reading sections before I was instructed to do so. I discovered that day that political slogans were like shoes, to be worn depending on the season or terrain. There are the shiny, the heavy, the supple, and the spurred. `Ali and I would get in trouble when we laughed during the meetings. The comrade threw us out once, yelling behind us, "No one forced you to join the Party!" We started to skip meetings to play soccer.

Later, a fire broke out in the office of the National Iraqi Student Union and destroyed all of their files. The comrades returned to the classrooms the next day to ask all of the members to stand in order to re-record their names. `Ali suggested that we stay sitting in order to get out of the meetings, and I agreed. And so we returned to the ranks of the independent. Some would later try to "win us," but we always refused. I remained independent, even after it was threatened that I wouldn't be accepted into a Master's program if I didn't join. But, "all good workers are sons of the revolution, and Ba`thists even if they don't join the Party."*

I wasn't in a mood to talk to anyone that day. A large banner hanging on the iron gates read: "The Soldiers of the Leader Compose Another Epic." A dean left the college for the balcony, and with him a group of aides. He walked forward and stood in front of the microphone to give one of his speeches. The media had announced the army's success in warding off a crippling attack, causing the enemy tens of thousands of casualties. Yet cars draped in flags had already begun to arrive from the front, announcing the size of our own losses that military updates did not disclose. A few months into the war, they had acquired the habit of omitting any mention of our casualties. The dean himself had obtained his

---

*A saying of our great Leader.

post two years earlier after he had showered the cultural pages of the newspapers with excerpts from his "Verses on the Battle," which was anything but verse. I felt nauseated whenever I heard these speeches, and would try to withdraw into my own world where nothing reached me but the sound of applause that followed certain magical words: Leader . . . Party . . . Revolution. I would stand with my hands in my pockets—I had stopped clapping sometime in high school as a method of silent protest—despite the warnings of those around me that they were reporting anyone who didn't applaud. Ra'ad, who played street soccer with us growing up, had disappeared, they say, because he didn't clap. I, of course, have a permanent excuse in my weak left hand—after all, one hand alone cannot clap!

That day you were standing alone. An island of silence amidst a sea of slogans, you paid no attention to this circus, and read a magazine. I knew you from French classes. You had caught my attention our first year, but you were in a different section. This year my name appeared on your list, and we attended the same lecture. I began to try to sit near you, and while the rest of the students practiced declining verbs in the various tenses I would practice pronouncing the details of your body in the present. I would memorize the lines of your body with the voracity of a child learning to speak. When I could only find a seat behind you, I began a liturgy from your earlobe, usually pierced with a silver earring whose simple elegance betrayed the wealth you tried to hide, to your smooth neck, down your arm to the silver bracelets that danced like a band of gypsies around your wrist when you raised your hand to answer a question. Then there was "the waist whose line was drawn in my dreams," as Nizar says.

I would recite the nudity restrained by your clothes, and your perfume would paint my mornings a land-scape of desire. You dropped a car key one morning while you gathered your books at the end of a lecture. I bent to pick it up, but you were faster. The collar of your blouse yielded as you bent, and I saw the land that lay between the two rivers, fenced at the banks by black silk. Seeing them so tightly bound, I could almost hear the cries of those two prisoners, and my eyes gasped in silence. But you rose, smilingly, and thanked me. With a restraint that contradicted my thoughts, I replied coolly, "You're welcome." Later, I reproached myself for not talking to you. I had been thinking of you for weeks, but had never been quick enough to approach you as you rushed from the lecture hall. Here you are now, alone, reading this week's *al-Yawm al-Sabi'* that I hadn't bought. I had sent them some poems several weeks before that they had yet to publish. It was a perfect excuse to talk to you, so I gathered my courage and walked in your direction.

"Hi, I'm Furat. I'm in your French class."

"Hi," you said.

"Sorry to bother you, but could I just see your magazine for a minute? I want to check something, and I haven't had time to buy it this week."

"Of course!" You smiled, and handed me the magazine. I flipped through the pages looking for the cultural section, and found the two pieces that I sent in the right-hand corner, set in beautiful type. I felt the stirring of an elation that might burst forth, even though this was the second time they'd published something of mine.

"Could I just read this page?" I asked.

"Sure," you said. Then, pointing to the page, you added, "Isn't that your name?"

"Yeah, it is."

"Congratulations. So, that means the rumor is true?"

"Which rumor?"

"That you write."

"News travels fast these days."

"And what's wrong with that? Is there something wrong with writing?"

"No," I said, "on the contrary."

"I bought it this morning, but I haven't had time to read it. I just saw your name and thought I should encourage a classmate. Why don't you read it to me?" I was stunned. My heart began to applaud in ecstasy as I began:

The two trees had stretched to reach each other more than once, but the district workers would cut their branches as reproof for their suspect union. And when it was decided that an asphalt carpet would be laid between them, the hungry saw did not linger long inside of their bodies before they fell into a passionate embrace, and turned their conversation toward their pallid future.

The autumn had overwhelmed the city, dispensing sadness along its streets. As for him, autumn visited his house four times a year. But that morning in particular he felt as if sadness had permeated everything. Even his tea tasted miserable. He looked at the clock splayed on his bedroom wall. The hour hand was sluggish, as was its custom, and the second hand spun around recklessly. He left a small sheet of paper on his desk after he had written: Goodbye, it's a losing game. He walked out onto the balcony and looked over the city from its towering height. He knew that he would never be able to fly, but the sidewalk accepted his resignation from life.

"They're beautiful," you said. "But sad. Is all of your work like this?"

"I don't know. I never really thought about it." I handed you back the magazine.

"Keep it," you said. "It's your work, after all."

"On one condition. That I pay you for it."

"No!" you cried. "It's a gift. You writers need financial support, don't you?"

"And moral support. Are you in the business of supporting writers?"

"Yes," you laughed. "I am a veritable institution." You laughed again, and I rejoiced from my depths. Here I am, near you, after weeks of waiting. The dean finished his speech, and the president of the Student Union directed us toward the main gate where we were to join the usual groups of students from the neighboring colleges. The warmth in your voice said, "It looks like we're moving."

We walked together and talked about classes and literature. You said you liked poetry — both old and new, and asked me what I liked. I answered that I like a lot of things, but what came to mind just then were, the *Mu'allaqat*, Abu Nuwas, al-Sayyab, Adunis, Mahmud Darwish, al-Jawahiri, and al-Nawwab. You raised your eyebrows at the last two, most likely because they were banned, if only unofficially. You said you knew al-Jawahiri and that "baba" likes his poetry, and that you had heard of Muzaffar al-Nawwab but never read anything by him. I promised to lend you one of his cassettes, and you asked me if I were one of those people who were enamored of forbidden objects. I answered that the forbidden was always more interesting, and you laughed. When we got to the main gate, the students from the other colleges had already massed in the outer courtyard that separates the college from the street. The gates were locked to prevent students from sneaking out. Banners and flags were distributed, and cameras were brought to film the event. At night, footage of these crowds of students rallying around their leadership were distributed and sent out to the world, where experts and analysts would compete to explain to their honorable audiences the mystery of our love for tyranny.

You sighed and said you would suffocate in this crowd.

"I'm going to try to get out. Are you staying?"

"No — why? Do I look like I'm enjoying myself?"

"You? Of course not. Let's go see if we can leave."

We cleaved a path through the crowd of students, who were radiating signs of discomfort. Before we got to the gate that emptied onto the street, we saw a group of our classmates walking toward us. "Don't bother," one of them said, "they're not letting anyone out." You looked at your watch. I asked you if you had somewhere to be. You said you had an appointment with your eye doctor, that you had developed an allergy to your contact lenses.

"Maybe we can explain the situation to one of the guards," I said. I thought that eyes like these should never have to be tired by contact lenses, and that the company who manufactures them should be blacklisted. The guard we approached was convinced by your excuse — or maybe it was your eyes — but wouldn't let me leave with you.

"See you tomorrow," you promised, smiling widely.

I waved my hand and watched you walk away toward the parking lot, and then returned to the courtyard. I took stock of the afternoon's developments; my profits appeared substantial — you were as sensitive and intelligent as I imagined you to be. I re-read my two pieces and silently replayed our conversation, especially those promising words: see you tomorrow.

Unraveling from the whiteness of the page, suns emerge tearing through the darkness of this night, recalling another galaxy. But they are captive suns, these others, trapped behind bar after bar. As if these lines were cords, or barbed wire upon which the words perch like frightened birds stalked by hunters or an approaching warden. Will they leave me to nest in others' branches, and fly in others' skies? Or will they be devoured by predators? I see them alight, one after the other, on this line. But they flee whenever I extend my trembling fingers. Every line bears the trace of a bar.

I awoke to find myself (t)here.

I was crouched in front of a wall of this vast nightmare, holding my ear against it. I heard a humming and a choked groan. I beat the wall with what was left of my strength and screamed as loudly as I could, "*Who's there?*" I pushed my fingernails into the wall and began to dig, crumbs of the nightmare mixing with my blood, saliva, and tears. I thought I could feel my nails about to reach the emptiness, and pulled them back, beating the wall with my fists until a hole opened large enough to peer into . . . a neighboring nightmare. I saw myself, crouched in front of a vast wall, holding my ear against it . . .

"Why don't you come with me to church? Maybe God will enlighten you."

"I don't want to be enlightened, *bibi*. I'm looking forward to hell. Leave me alone, please."

"What is this? You talk like you're a hundred years old. You're still a child."

Where is she now? Praying to an idea, just as she has done every day for half a century. Kneeling before a statue of the Virgin and praying to her crucified son.

"Where do you go? You leave the house in the morning and don't come back until after dark. Do you go roaming the alleys? One of those Ba`thi boys came here today to ask why we don't have a picture of the President on our wall."

"What did you tell him?"

"He was just a child, younger than you. He couldn't have been older than twenty. I told him I put it with Maryam for her to protect him." She insisted on hanging a large picture of the Virgin Mary in the sitting room. She also insisted on placing a photo of the president beneath it. She said it was better to keep a small photo of him so we didn't give the sons of bitches a chance to report us. "He told me, 'Hang a bigger one, auntie.' "

"That's it?"

"No. He was filling out forms, and asked me if there were any Party members living in the house."

"But it's just you and me in the house."

"I know, I told him my son—well, my son's son, I mean—isn't a member, and I'm an old woman. I told him, do you mean to tell me that I should spend my last years going to meetings?"

"What did he say?"

"He said, 'Auntie, your people need to put a brick in this country's edifice.' "

"No! You should have told him that 'all good workers are sons of the revolution, and Ba`thists even if they don't join the Party.' "

"I told him we've been in this country for thousands of years. Why should we have to put up a brick?"

My grandmother always took pride in our Chaldean origins, and would get angry when I would try to convince her that, culturally, we were Arabs—or Arabized, at least, and not a separate ethnicity like the Armenians or Assyrians. Or when I would say that all that is left of Chaldea is the language used in Mass—the one she speaks with relatives of her generation or with me when she is angry—and even that is dying out. She would always refuse to discuss the subject and accuse me of abandoning my heritage.

"Shut your mouth! Now you're not making any sense! How can you forget your roots?"

My memory attacks me and uproots the barbed wire separating here from there. The borders and "forbidden" signs piercing my skin disappear. Red clouds pass by overhead, overpowering the cringing sun. Children burst laughing from my skull, opening their schoolbags and ripping apart the books imprisoned inside. They make airplanes of their pages and scrawl angry slogans on the walls that stretch in every direction. The past advances quickly toward the present. They collide. Their shards scatter.

I awake to find myself (t)here.

We were walking near the university one dark, autumn day, when I asked you, "What's your favorite season?"

"Fall. You?"

"The final season."

"What?" you said with surprise, turning toward me.

"Well, if I told you fall, you'd think I was just trying to please you, and that I didn't have a personality of my own."

"What's with the false modesty? Since when do you doubt your personality? Agh, do you never get tired of praise? I thought we'd grown out of the phase of flattery, and begun to be honest, to break down the boundaries."

I, myself, had begun to fear that we knew each other too well, and that the initial, beautiful moments of infatuation were passing. But I could always rely on my madness to combat problems like these.

"Of course, I support the breaking of chains, unity, freedom, socialism, and a whole host of like synonyms, not to mention the defense of our noble cause." You nodded and looked at the watch on your right hand.

"Look, we're late. But it seems that you're prepared for the National Hemorrhage* lecture," she said, referring to my sophistry.

"By the way," I asked. "Why do you wear your watch on your right hand?"

"Because I'm not as left as you are, my dear sir! Listen, enough. We have to make it to the lecture. I can't afford another absence. I used to be a good student, you know, before I met you."

"So you regret it?"

"What's going on? Why can't you take a joke? You've been in a shitty mood lately."

"I just don't want to go to the National Hemorrhage[†] lecture."

In order to reach the department, we had to walk around an enclosure with high brick walls. I had always wondered what was hidden inside this place that people called a garden. One of the walls was the elevated rail track, but the other three were brick and cement, too high to allow anyone to see what they hid behind them. Once, while I was waiting for the bus, I tried to climb the track, but found a fence preventing me from reaching the platform. Unusually, the gate was open that day.

---

*National Heritage?

[†] Heritage?

"We'll be on time if we walk in a straight line," I said, pointing to the gate. You agreed.

We crossed a short entryway surrounded by trees, and found ourselves before an unexpected sight. The "garden" consisted of hundreds of white tombstones, organized into rows on green, carefully trimmed grass. Each stone bore a name written in English, followed by a military rank and dates of birth and death, along with a phrase like "Rest in Peace," or "Gone But Not Forgotten." It was clear from the names and dates that these were British soldiers who had died during the invasion of Iraq in 1917. The graves were laid according to military rank.

"Look there!" you said. You pointed to the right, where in a corner there perched a small marble statue that appeared to be the unit commander.

"Can you imagine, I spent three years wondering what this place was, and never once imagined it was a cemetery full of British soldiers!"

"Do you think that's why they put this wall here — so no one would see it?"

"I don't know. I mean, what could happen? Didn't we get rid of the English a long time ago?"

"Sure, but it looks like this wall was built in the forties or fifties, when the government and the British were still 'two asses with one hole.' They must have been afraid of demonstrations."

"Yeah, but now the time of the British has passed. It's the age of America, and it's not like they'll occupy us."

"Well, let's just get rid of the Iranians for now, thank you." We laughed, and you pointed to the door leading to the street, leading to campus.

"Come on, quick," you said. But then you added, "Look how young they were. Eighteen, nineteen. *Haram*, it's a shame."

"You traitor, you're sympathizing with the occupiers."

"No, seriously. Isn't it sad?" Before we had a chance to discuss the ethics of war, a man emerged from a small shed we hadn't noticed in the corner of the cemetery.

"Hey! What are you doing here? It's forbidden!"

"Forbidden" was the most often-used word in the country, especially among those who enjoyed a bit of power, or imagined they did. This man was protecting his own small empire—filled with those fallen in the service of another.

"Why is it forbidden?" I challenged him.

"Shame on you, this is a cemetery!"

"What, you think we're grave robbers?"

"Son, this is my job. I'm under orders."

You asked him in a less antagonistic tone, "Do you work here, sir?"

"Yes, I'm the caretaker."

"Who comes here?"

"Ambassadors sometimes come and bring wreaths."

"Which ambassadors?" I asked.

"Australia, England, Canada, I don't know!"

We had already walked halfway across the cemetery, so we asked him if he could open the second gate for us to leave. He walked with us toward the gate, and pleaded with us, "Please, by God, don't do it again. You'll make trouble for me. I'm supposed to close the door tight." We reassured him that we wouldn't come again, and he thanked us, locking the door behind us as we left.

"Did you know I love cemeteries?"

"You never told me so, but I'm not surprised," you said.

I was obsessed with the idea of death, and asked you with all seriousness, "Do you think that on the Day of Reckoning those soldiers will be judged together, or with their families? I mean, what's the order of affiliation?"

"That's a good question. I don't know. Does that mean you believe in the Day of Reckoning?"

"No. I mean, only as an idea."

"I don't know, and I don't care either right now. What I care about is making that lecture. You know my father will go crazy if I get suspended for absences."

"Ha!" I laughed, "You answered my question! The family, as an institution, is stronger than all the armies of the world."

"Maybe for the English soldiers it wasn't, but for our society, unfortunately, it is."

"*Zayn*. If there turns out to be a day of reckoning, do you think you and I'll be judged together?"

"Don't worry—I'll look for you."

"But won't the morality commission summon us

once they discover the crimes we've committed, sleeping together without a social or religious contract?"

"I'm sure they will, but there must be some bureaucrat we can bribe."

"Maybe you can sleep with one of the angels so he'll stamp our souls 'heaven.'"

"And if the angel likes boys will you agree to sleep with him?" you asked, laughing.

"I'll have to think about it."

"You'll have to think about it? Where is your feminism? Your radicalism? I can use my body for your salvation, but not yours for mine?"

"Darling, liberation from social constructs takes time. I'm prepared to mount him if wants me to, but I'm not prepared to be fucked."

"It takes time? How long? In a few years you'll get older and more conservative. You're just like all the others. All slogans and no action. Who knows, maybe the angel will be gentle with you."

I imagined myself mounted on the back of an angel, touring the grounds of heaven. . . .

We walked toward the mural of the Leader that hung in front of the Party headquarters. Two young men holding machine guns guarded the entrance, and the Leader presided over them in sunglasses, waving to a crowd of people whose faces had been left blurred by the painter. I remembered what happened the last time we walked by. You had admired one of the yellow roses that were planted in the garden beneath the mural. I told you I'd go pick it.

"No," you said. "I don't want it. It's part of the display."

"Come on, there's no one here."

The roaches were inside that day. I hurried to pluck the rose, and when I returned to where you stood on the sidewalk I heard a voice behind me scream, "Hey! What are you doing?"

The speaker was about my age, with coffee-colored eyes sunk into a rectangular face. Before I could venture an answer he said in a stiff tone, as if he had caught us in the act of a crime, "Come here! Why did you do that?"

You hurried to save the situation. "I told him to."

"What, are we running a nursery here? These are for the display, and not every passer-by. If you want romance, go buy flowers from a store."

It seemed that the comrade was unaware of the current rose crisis and their monstrous prices. I told him with a bit of arrogance, "I didn't know it wasn't allowed."

You added, "Its my fault. I'm the one who asked him for it. I'm sorry." There was silence for a few seconds, then he added, like a teacher lecturing his students, "Okay, just don't do it again. You're not children, are you?"

You thanked him for his "kindness" and dragged me away by my arm. You accused me of being reckless, and of getting us into an absurd situation just to prove something even more absurd. I admired your composure. You tried to comfort me, saying you would keep the rose forever.

"It's the most dangerous rose I've ever gotten."

You said it reminded you of the Russian cartoon we often watched on state television, where the hero attempts to steal a jewel from between the eyes of a sleeping dragon for his beloved. The difference was that, in the Russian cartoon, the hero strikes down the monster, while our pride is all that was stricken. Our monster remains asleep, and instead his dogs bark at us.

You interrupted my memories to ask what I was thinking about.

"Roses."

"Which roses?"

"Don't you remember the farce of the roses, in front of the Party headquarters?"

"Come on, there aren't any more roses."

"By the way, do you know why our Heritage professor threw that student out of class a couple of weeks ago?"

"Just how did you make that discovery?"

"Don't you want to know what the discovery is first?"

"Sure, but I also want to know how."

"I'll give you three hours to guess, and if you don't get it I'll tell you. The answer comes from poetry — poetry is the answer to all questions."

"You are the king of contradictions. Yesterday you told me that poetry *asks* every question in the world."

"I changed my mind. Now think! Why did the professor throw out the student who wore a red rose in her lapel?"

"I remember we thought about it all day, but we couldn't figure it out."

The course in National Hemorrhage* was the only one required for all university students, whether they were majoring in Russian literature or veterinary science. We would assemble in a large lecture hall for two hours every week, where we would study the Ba`thist ideology and those grand theories of `Aflaq and Elias Farah. Then, in our third year with the war, the Leader's speeches and sayings, which were often published in pamphlets, became a regular part of the curriculum. You and I usually sat in the last row and passed notes, or read. Especially that year, because the professor never asked the students questions in class, preferring to theorize. He was kind in comparison to the previous year's instructor; he would touch upon international events and was light-hearted. And so we were shocked when he had erupted in anger two weeks earlier and ordered a student in the front row to leave the classroom and get rid of the red rose she had pinned to her lapel.

"What's this? Sitting here so proud of your red rose! Get out!"

The student hurried out of the room, wiping her tears in front of nearly two hundred students. We saw him talking to her politely after class that day.

"Do you think he was a bull in a previous life, and still gets agitated by the color red?" you suggested, laughing. I told you I was sure that wasn't the reason.

---

*National Heritage?

"Then go ahead, tell me. We'll get to class any minute."

"Yesterday I was reading al-Jawahiri and saw a poem called 'Salam' that he recited at the anniversary celebration of the Communist party on March 31, and that day was also the 31st of March."

"But is it the poor student's fault that they're still terrified of the Communist party? Haven't they gotten rid them all, anyway?" You lowered your voice when you pronounced the last question. "I'm sure she didn't know. Who in our generation knows anything about the Communist party except that they're 'traitors?' All I remember are those twenty officers that were hanged at the end of the seventies."

"Sure, but the professor must have been afraid that if he didn't tell her to take off the flower they would write him up. It would be an opportunity for someone to prove that they're a loyal and unresting eye for the Party."

We had walked onto the university grounds through the main gate, and turned left toward al-Farahidi Hall. The professor had not yet arrived. After we found two neighboring seats at the back, as we always did, I wrote down the poem I had memorized on a page of *The Old Man and the Sea* that we were reading for another class. Some of its lines are still clear in my mind:

From time immemorial
When the fields became green
With dark-skinned desires

When masters ruled over slaves
The earth inhaled the winds of struggle
And the vagrant's forehead rested on mountaintops
Precious blood inundated the earth
Thirsty, timid nails were hammered
Into men's palms and blood splashed
Onto the foreheads of later epochs

Chains were molded and skins made whips
And men dangled from treetops
The sun rose with a tear on its cheek

Struggle alighted in a land
Where blood waters the sand
Where reality wrestles with fantasy
On the banks of Tigris and the Euphrates
Where the have-nots fall
As they change the world*

The Communist party had been slaughtered long years ago. Its nose was amputated and its eyes gouged, then it was torn limb from limb and left to desiccate in prisons and exile. Of course, there were those who were weak and preferred to join the long Ba`thist carnival that would follow. The Party's anniversary was but a forgotten grave—yet even a red rose, mistakenly placed on its tombstone, was enough to cause them terror.

The only communist in our family was my second

---

*I found the entire poem in al-Jawahiri's collected works.

cousin, Elias. He was a "follower of Tito," according to what I heard when I was young, and was responsible for all of the Baghdad cells. He spent some time in prison, and even after his release was under surveillance for over a year. I remember him coming to visit one Easter and telling us over my grandmother's fig jam (she was a jam virtuoso) the story of the security officer assigned to follow him. He told us how the officer followed him by motorcycle wherever he went for an entire year, and how one day he invited the officer to eat dinner with him, because he said he could sense the inconvenience of his task. "It must have kept the man from his family," my cousin said. That was years ago, though. Today, they prefer to extend a dubious invitation to you, rather than tire themselves in your pursuit!

I lay nude on my back on top of the white sand and below the deep black sky. The moon hiding behind a dark cloud began to shed drops the color of ink. I felt the cold drops dotting my body and wiped one that had fallen on my forehead, and another that rested on my chest. My fingers blackened. A howl reached my ears from the distance. I rose and looked around me, but saw only the inky rain that spotted the sand, whose rhythm had sped up into a downpour. I heard the howl nearing, followed by barking and the roar of what sounded like an engine. Fear seized me and propelled me in the opposite direction. The shower became a deluge, and the rain began to gather into small lakes that I would jump over as I ran with all of my strength. I fell, and the rain-blackened sand stained my cheeks, my chest, my thighs. I wiped my face and rose again, running away from the howling and roaring. I turned, looking for the source of the sounds, and saw my footsteps writ clearly on the white sand. I thought about burying myself in it and hiding. But the dogs, whose howling and barking now approached, would smell me. I ran and ran until fatigue overcame me, and I fell, panting, on my face. The roaring stopped, and I heard the opening and closing of car doors and footsteps. Suddenly, bright lights appeared, coming from flashlights held in the hands of men leading the dogs. I ran again between the bars of light, and heard their footsteps running behind me. After a short while the cold and fatigue overcame me, and I collapsed again. The parallel bars of light lit the entire desert. The men released their dogs. They ran along the blinding rays. I tried to stand again and run, but I felt an unbearable pain in my feet and head. I crawled, like an animal searching for a place to die. The barking was close by. I turned to find a dog ready to pounce. Its fangs shone, and I saw its pink gums lined with black. I hid my head behind my hands. I opened my eyes to find the white page in front of me, with its black lines stretching out from my head. Do I write?

I was always reciting al-Jawahiri when I was with Areej so I could impress her with how much of his poetry I knew. She told me that if he knew how much I recited his work he would make me his publicist. One day she told me she had a surprise for me. Her father had bought a video recording of an interview with al-Jawahiri on Abu Dhabi television.

"Want to see it?"

"I'd love to."

"We can eat lunch at my house and watch it, and be back in time for the French lecture at four."

"But what about your family?"

"There's no one at home. My mother is out and baba is traveling."

"But isn't there a travel ban? He must have connections."

"He got permission to go to a conference in Italy. Plus, even if they were home, they're open-minded. What, are you scared?" she laughed.

"Why should I be? I'm just worried about your reputation."

"Better worry about your own reputation."

"Bravo!"

"Do you like eggplant? I made some yesterday."

"It's the first time you invite me to your house and you serve me leftovers?"

"Darling, if I knew you were coming ahead of time I would have slaughtered you a lamb. Now, forgive me this time?"

We didn't talk much in the car on the way to her house in al-Kazimiyya, as if we were both thinking about the afternoon's possibilities. Or perhaps it was the effect of the melancholy music she was playing; she loved Chopin's nocturnes. I asked her about the evil eye talisman hanging from her rear-view mirror. She said she hung it for purely aesthetic reasons, and that she doesn't really believe in those kinds of things. She told me I was always looking for something to criticize, and I suggested she get together with my grandmother and form a faction against me. The road passed through a poor area filled with small houses, but with a small strip looking over the Tigris filled with tall buildings. They gave the impression of wealth that comes with that aesthetic sense that has been lost on the homes of the nouveau riche, which have sprung to the surface since the war began. We passed some children playing soccer in the street, having flung their backpacks on the ground. She smiled and waved at them, and they ran behind the car for a few meters, screaming and laughing.

The paved street turned into a winding dirt road and ended in an iron gate. I offered to get out and open it, and she agreed with a smile and "How sweet you are!" I opened the gate and stood aside as the car entered the driveway and stopped in front of the kitchen window. We went in the kitchen door, and she dropped her books on the kitchen table.

"Come in. Do you want to eat first or watch the video?"

"Whatever you want," I said.

"Both! I'll heat up the food, and you can go relax in the living room. Look at the books, or the garden. I know you love the river."

"Do you need help?"

"No, *tislam*."

A hallway connected the kitchen to the living room. The walls were covered with paintings by famous artists, like Ali Talib, Layla al-`Attar, and Fa'iq Hassan. One wall was completely covered with bookshelves. I read their titles. Many were books about architecture — Islamic architecture, English architecture, French architecture. There were volumes of classical Arabic poetry — al-Mu`allaqat, al-Hamasa, al-Mufaddaliyyat. I saw *The Book of Songs*, and collections of al-Mutanabbi and Abu Nuwas. I opened the glass door leading to the garden and stepped outside, closing it behind me. A white swing hung on one side, next to a white iron table and chairs that stood on the carefully cut grass. A small bed of roses hugged the edge of the garden. I walked toward the river and descended the spiral staircase leading to its banks. The Tigris was running calmly, paying no attention to the absurdity and death at its shores, or the palaces that had begun to stab at its banks. Of course, there were no boats floating on it. A decree had been announced several years ago banning river traffic. The unacknowledged reason was that the Leader and his retinue's castles had clogged the river's banks. One could sometimes see a small fishing boat, but that was all. I bent to stroke the river—the water was cold. I thought that the drops on my hand might have come from ice on the mountains of Turkey, or a cloud that ended its life in the mountains of Kurdistan. I repeated al-Sayyab's question to the Tigris: "Are you a river or a forest of tears?"

I heard her voice calling me inside, so I turned back. We sat on a couch in front of the television, eating and watching the interview. Al-Jawahiri talked about his childhood in Najaf, and the oppressive regime that drove him out of the country, and how he had memorized thousands of lines of poetry before he had written a line of his own. There was an unacknowledged interdiction against him because of his position against the war. They couldn't excise his immortal poetry like "Farewell" from school textbooks, but his name had not been uttered publicly since he left the country in 1980. Some of his poems were smuggled in on cassette tapes that we would trade secretly in school. He talked about the difficulties of his exile in Prague, and how lately the situation has been turned upside down, and exile has become his homeland. The interview ended with him reciting a love poem—proving that he is even a master of longing. I had put my hand on yours while we watched, and you held it hotly. Your perfume drifted into my pores and migrated through my arteries. When the interview ended, you rose to eject the cassette and turn off the television. You asked me if I liked it, and when you were certain of my satisfaction you promised to make me a copy. You came back and sat next to me again, facing me. You brushed a lock of hair that was covering your eye back behind your ear. You leaned your head on the couch, and the down of your neck shone. You folded your knees onto the couch. You smiled.

"Do you want tea?"

"No, thanks."

"What do you want, then?"

"A lot."

"Like what?"

"I want to kiss you."

You smiled again and moved your face close to mine. The smile in your eyes encouraged me. I put my fingers on your cheek and imprinted a light kiss on your mouth. I followed it with another, longer one, while I folded my arms around you. Your lower lip snuck between mine and lingered shortly before it disentangled itself. My lips crawled to your cheek, then to your neck, to your earlobe. I bit it softly, and you laughed and set free a trapped sigh. I descended to your neck again, and then your throat. I sowed kisses on your chest. And when I reached my hand to open your blouse you took it in yours. I thought you were stopping me, but you pulled my hand instead and stood up from the couch, saying, "Come."

You took me to the hallway leading to the other side of the house. I was going to enter the first door, but you pulled me on.

"That's my parents' room!"

"So what?"

"Pervert!"

You laughed coquettishly. Your room was the last in the hallway. You closed the curtains. We peeled the clothes off each other while engrossed in a long kiss. I felt the cool of your palms on my back. I rubbed my mouth between your breasts and began to kiss them. They were firm and a little bigger than I had imagined. I kissed your left nipple and bit it gently, and you trembled, pulling my hair and moaning. My tongue crept to your right nipple, and then again to the left, circling it with my tongue. You asked me, between breaths, why I paid more attention to your left breast than your right, but I could find no answer.

"Do you have the Oedipus complex?"

You laughed and pulled me to the bed. You lay beneath me, and I kissed the land between the two rivers and descended slowly toward your navel and stroked it with my tongue.

"Don't tickle!"

I continued my descent toward the delta, but you grabbed my hands and raised me to you. We shared a deep kiss, so warm I felt it invade my bones. Then you pushed me aside and I found myself on my back with you on top of me. You grabbed my hands and held them on my sides, strangling my body with your thighs. Your breasts hung like two clusters of grapes and your nipples smiled on my cheeks. We clung together in a rhythm that sped in unison, until our sweat was intermingled.

I awoke to find myself (t)here.

The white of the page seduces me with the freedom to wander in my isolation. I will shatter the surface of this silence with my delirium. Words have turned into legendary beings, digging a tunnel to the outside, or prisms I hang all around me to look through.

Anxiously, I drew a question mark and sat looking at it for hours. It returned my gaze. Then, suddenly, it stood on its dot, shivering and saying, "I give myself to you, so take me and make of me what you'd like! I will be a scythe with which you can reap the doubt that gnaws at you. Or sow me where you like, and I will grow to protect you from them." I grabbed it by its waist, and it was as pliant as clay. I turned it on its head, flattened the curve of its waist, and stretched its dot into an angular *hamza*. It became the letter *kaf*.

Why write? Why should I not write? To write or not to write. Am I here because someone wrote about me? I'll gouge the eye of anyone who dares try to read me!

They wrote me in here, or I wrote myself here, and I will write my pain* out. My back has curved. I fold like a question mark to gather the scattered pieces of myself

---

*way

and then withdraw into my dark tunnel. "They'll throw you inside." Ali was right. "Don't be an idiot! Just shut up. Otherwise, they'll stick it up your ass."

"Please keep quiet son."

I went to buy the newspapers, as usual, and saw the new edition of *al-Yawm al-Sabi*. I had sent them a new piece I'd written and was anxious to see if they had published it. I took a copy, and when I gave the money to the storeowner he asked me for more. When I asked him why he told me that there was a pamphlet sold with it. I opened the magazine and found a copy of "Speech of the President on the Transformation of Workers into Employees."

"But I don't want it," I explained.

"If you want *al-Yawm al-Sabi*, then you have to buy it."

"Man, I told you I don't want it. I just want the magazine."

"Sorry, they're sold together."

I refused and returned the magazine and pamphlet to him, and decided to buy it from another stand. He grumbled, putting the pamphlet back inside the magazine and handed me back my money.

"What are we going to do? They force us to take them, and we can't return them."

I realize now that the storeowner looked a lot like Ahmad. Will these words ever leave the isolation of these pages? Or will they meet their end in the belly of a fat rat? Why did they give me these papers? Is it a new game they've invented? Can I trust him? Can I trust my instincts, which got me here in the first place? Will I be able to keep these papers? They are not the first . . . I tore those up and swallowed them, afraid of what might happen if they were found.

The announcer looked out from the door and said, "Can we have your attention, please? We are about to make an important announcement." He disappeared, and then reappeared after two songs.

"Ladies and gentlemen, an official spokesman has made the following announcement: Children of the homeland and nation, after a fierce war fought by our fearless army and led by the Knight of the Nation, Hero of Peace and Victory, the evil enemy forces have been defeated. By the wisdom of our inspired Leader and by the historic bravery of our soldiers, you have protected the nation from peril. Light has prevailed over darkness, and transparency reigns in all parts of the country. Your proud soldiers have uprooted the last remnants of uncertainty and doubt, and a new era of justice and clarity has dawned. In order to protect the nation and the coming generations from the evil of the enemy, our Leader has issued a decree calling for the confiscation of those lexicons and dictionaries distributed by the enemy in an attempt to sow the seeds of discord among our people. You are invited to burn these at one of the celebrations taking place all over the country, where our great people will celebrate their readiness to greet the new time of consensus, which this rabble has tried to violate. The Leader has also ordered the Ministry of the Interior to distribute to every citizen a list of essential words and their meanings in order that we are able to preserve our hard-earned clarity of meaning. Instructions have also been issued to the Ministry of Education to make these words part of the basic curriculum of elementary education. Also published is a list of titles for the Leader, and the rules for their proper use. All foreign languages are banned, as are local dialects that encourage separatists and enemies of the nation (except the dialect of our President, which has been declared by the National Congress to be an official dialect, by virtue of the eloquence and splendor God has bestowed in it). The National Regress*, who are your diacritically† elected representatives, have declared that the punishment for publishing vaguery or ambiguity, or the violation of clear meaning (for which our brave martyrs have sacrificed their blood), should be elocution.‡ Hearings will be set up to try anyone who should commit the crime of illegal individual interpretation, and official committees of interpretation will be set up as a coordinated effort of the Ministries of Culture and Interior in order to delineate the suitable guidelines for interpreting texts. The importation of foreign contexts is categorically banned. Let the outcasts be cast out!"

---

*Congress?

† Democratically?

‡ Execution?

Every day she would walk to the Church of the Sacred Heart, and on holidays or during the month of Lent, she would go to Our Lady of Sorrows in the Christian quarter of Baghdad, and tell me she would be late getting home. I used to love that church because she took me there as a child. I loved the gravity of the rituals and the incense, in that time before books would steer me far from faith. I still remember the stork's nest that perched on top of its dome. Inside, I took my first communion, which was supposed to make a direct entry into my heart. Inside also, "our father" washed my feet with a group of other young boys, as the Lord had done with his apostles. At first I refused to participate in this ritual, but she made me swear by the memory of my father that I would participate. But "our father" did not kiss my feet as Christ did with his apostles, but sufficed with bringing his lips within centimeters of my newly scrubbed toes. My grandmother was angry when I told her of the fugitive kiss and accused me of making the story up. Isn't "our father," after all, Christ's representative on earth? That was the beginning of our difference of opinion regarding the church and its men. She also got angry when I refused to kiss the Archbishop's ring when he visited us on Christmas. She told me I would only be kissing the ring on his hand, a symbol, and not the hand itself.

The history of the country lumbered forward while my grandmother attended church. When King Ghazi was killed, she was in Our Lady of Sorrows—because my grandfather's house was in the Christian quarter at that time—and during the movement of Rashid 'Ali al-Gaylani she was in Sacred Heart, and when the Ba'thists took power she was in Karradat Maryam. I used to tell her that she should go to church once a week on Sundays, like everyone else, and not every day. But the seven weekly meetings continued, leaving a clear mark in her white hair and weak constitution. After the death of my parents in a car accident when I was seven, she raised me, and she always complained that God should have taken her instead. Despite her constant complaints about the situation, which became harsher if the price of fruits and vegetables rose, she would blame fate for everything and was convinced that matters were always getting worse.

"You think whoever comes next will be any better? These people need to be ruled with an iron hand."

What angered her most, though, was the evening news that began to run over in order to report the activities of our intrepid Leader—delaying her favorite Egyptian soap operas for hours.

"What's going on?" she'd admonish the television, "Still?" I would tease her and try to convince her that the real shame was that the actors were all waiting in the studio for the Leader's diary to end, and she would look at me blankly, not knowing whether or not to believe me. "Well, you go and become President, and then we'll see what you do differently."

I returned home to find her drinking tea in front of the television, as usual.

"Just in time! Come drink this tea and watch."

Soldiers and officers were standing single-file around a hall, according to rank, each with a gold pin affixed to the lapel of their suits. They were ready to receive their medals of honor from the commander-in-chief, who was, coincidentally, also employed at the time as President of the Republic, Leader of the Revolutionary Council, Prime Minister, and Secretary-General of the Party. A commander entered from the right of the screen and shouted, "Preeeepare!" And they all prepared. The Leader then entered, flanked by his minister of defense and a number of generals and advisors. He walked past the rows of soldiers and stood in front of a big gilded chair, and his escorts dispersed to his right and left. The camera moved to the official spokesperson:

"In accordance with the outstanding bravery that these officers and their regimens have displayed in the protection of our nation's honor in our just battle against the brutal enemy, we have issued the following decree: The medal of honor of the highest degree shall be awarded to all those present . . ." The reading of the names then began. The Leader approached each soldier, and taking a medal from a tray held by an attendant, affixed it to a pin, and grabbed the bearer by the hand and moved it up and down, uttering a "Congratulations." He would then accept the soldier's gratitude. Some would turn their

heads to the side as a sign of respect, and he would sometimes ask the soldiers about their families or villages.
"Where is your family?" he might ask, and after the
answer he might respond, "Send them my regards."

As the war continued and the number of battles
increased, it became more common to receive these
medals, and they were sometimes awarded in bulk. Then
came the rank of "Friends of the President," for those
who had received three or more medals — their recipi-
ents were awarded special compensation, such as a car, or
a plot of land, or immunity from future prosecution. But
he would always congratulate everyone with the shake
of a hand. Then the tradition of storytelling began,
where soldiers would narrate their stories of heroism.

"Now, who is going to tell us a story today?" the
Leader would ask.

That day an officer stood in front of the microphone
used by the press secretary, gave his rank, unit and divi-
sion, and told his story. He recounted in great detail an
attack on an enemy position, and was careful to mention
that he was part of the advanced guard, despite his high
rank. The Leader interrupted (as he would often do in
order to clarify correct procedure), to say that despite
one's bravery it is the duty of high-ranking officers to
remain in the rear in order to more effectively direct the
operation. My grandmother apparently agreed:

"He's right," she told me. "It's true."

I reminded her that in an award ceremony some

months ago he had criticized an officer for staying in the rear, saying that officers must be the spearhead of an operation, in order to embolden the spirit of his soldiers. I reminded her that we were sitting right here, sitting and drinking tea just like this, when we heard him.

"I don't remember that. You just pulled that right out of your pocket, didn't you?"

"No, I swear to God."

"Don't you swear to God—I know you have no religion."

"You mean you'd rather I swore to Satan?"

"Father, son, and holy ghost! You know I don't like that kind of talk. Stop teasing me."

I heard the sound of a door opening in the darkness. An `alif fell through it, prancing and letting off a purple light. It stood in front of me and plucked the *hamza* from on top of its head, tipping it to me like a cap. He threw it behind him and plunged into the wall that had become a mirror. He bowed to me with respect and signaled to the *ba*, who was poking out his head, to enter. The *ba* came and bowed, and then went in, and behind him the *ta* and the *tha*. They all dropped their dots when they bowed, and afterward they would look in the mirror and laugh, dancing and spinning in giddy circles. Each of the letters of the alphabet followed: the *jim*, the *ha'* and the *kha'*, the *dal* and the *dhal*, the *ray* and the *zayn*, the *sin* and the *shin*.

The laughter rose and the dots fell, one after the other. The letters that take no dots began to pick them up from the ground and put them in their buttonholes or on their heads, or to stand on them and look at themselves in the mirror. One began to fight with the others, and stole their dots. The *sin* stole *shin's* dots and then raised its fingers to its lips, with a loud, "Shhhh!" The *mim* lay down on his stomach and raised his head to swallow the two dots he had picked up off the ground. A lustful laughter swelled up, and the letters danced together, coupling in forbidden positions. Then the mirror broke and soldiers raided the party, felling the letters with a spray of gunfire.

And I awoke to find myself (t)here.

"So, what's new in the papers?"

Her eyes were two bursts of bloom, shedding a scent of mint or giving off rays of sunshine on a languid day. The cold rain of her voice carried me far from the daily lies that the papers celebrated, and to which I was, unfortunately, addicted. She was wearing a white shirt with a beneficently open collar, a tight gray skirt that revealed her knees, and red shoes. She carried her blue jacket in her arms on top of her books. Not even the uniforms we were forced to wear could subdue her beauty. We were all to wear white shirts, bullet-colored pants (skirts for girls), and blue jackets. Some colleges were more lax about enforcing these orders, but ours was, for some reason, obsessed with the dress code and especially fanatical about enforcing the beard interdiction. The idea behind the uniform, as we were told, was to hide class differences among the students. This contradicted what we heard day and night, however: that the Revolution had already erased those differences, and that poverty no longer existed in our rich society. Yet the difference remained clear between those of us who wore locally made clothes and those whose family's wealth allowed them to buy expensive, imported clothes. With the appointment of the new Minister of Higher Education and Scientific Inquiry (who had never graduated high school), who was before this mayor of Baghdad and was rewarded with this new post for his accomplishment of cleaning up the city streets and speeding up garbage removal by personally beating the workers early every morning, the issue of school uniforms became sacred. He ordered professors to remove from class those students who did not comply. The person responsible for uniform enforcement in our college ran after those who disobeyed, grabbing them and throwing them bodily off the campus.

"The most important news of the day is that the Zawra' are playing Rashid."

"Are you one of those soccer fanatics?"

"Yeah, a veteran Zawra' fan. Why, you're not?"

"No. I watch the games that play on television."

"And you don't root for a particular team?"

"No, I'm neutral. But I do like Brazil."

"Who doesn't?"

I smiled and looked at my watch. Because I knew the effect of traffic on public transport, especially on days of important games, I realized that I would have to leave soon in order not to miss the starting whistle. I wished I could keep talking to her, but I hated missing seeing the team come out onto the field. So I said, with some regret in my voice, "You'll have to excuse me, but I have to leave to catch the game."

"And you're not going to invite me?" she asked. I was shocked by her question.

"Of course, I'd love it if you would, but I'm warning you there'll only be three or four girls in the entire stadium."

"Well, we'll have to change that, won't we?"

I was overjoyed, and picked my books up from the bench. "Absolutely," I said. "Let's go."

"We can take my car."

I knew that she had her own car because I'd seen her leaving school before, but I never thought I'd be riding in it so quickly. We got in the car and went south on the freeway toward the People's Stadium. She asked me to tell her the story of my obsession with the Zawra', and I felt the need to warn her that attending games was not as simple as it used to be. For since the "the ustadh," the President's son, established the Rashid team and was elected president of the Olympic committee (After the

Ministry of Youth was dissolved and the Olympic committee took its place, elections were held for president of the committee, but only the ustadh ran. He was unanimously elected.), the civilian workers that ran the stadium were replaced by the Palace Guard whenever the ustadh came to "observe" the games. He had also forced all of the best players to join his new team, with enticements at times and threats at others, until his team had become the best in the country, crowded with all the national stars.

The Rashid team enjoyed limitless financial support and was administratively linked to the Republican Palace. It was, truly, as one Egyptian spectator pointed out, "the government's team." Therefore, some would go to the games just to cheer against Rashid. One day the man sitting next to me asked if Kazim Wa'l would play that day. I reminded him that Wa'l had retired from the league years ago after his injury, and he told me "Oh well, the important thing is that we root against Rashid."

"Are you ready to chant against the government?" I asked her.

"If you chant, I'll chant. Just as long as you don't turn out to be one of them," she laughed.

"And how do I know that you aren't one of them? But I suppose I've already incriminated myself."

"True, you'd better watch out. But maybe you're just laying a trap for me, trying to make me talk. To steal my tongue."

"Heaven forbid."

I smiled and thought to tell her that stealing her tongue had been one of my primary goals since I first saw her. I liked her forwardness, especially at this early stage in our flirtation. I decided that I couldn't sit where I usually do, in the cheap open-air section, because she'd be harassed, so I suggested that we sit in the covered section even though it was much more expensive. "The seats in the covered section are more comfortable," I told her. The seats in the rest of the stadium were concrete benches that spectators would crowd into during important games. I remembered then that Falah would be waiting for me in our agreed place on the outside, but I was sure that he would understand after I explained the reason for my absence. We parked the car on the north side of the stadium, beneath another mural of the Father-Leader laughing with a group of Party leaders, his arm around one of them. The phrase "We win over the youth to guarantee the future" was painted beneath them. She asked if the car would be safe in this spot, and I answered quickly, "Don't worry about the car—he'll protect it."

"What is it with you? How do you know I'm not going to report that?" she said, adopting an authoritative tone.

"I trust you," I told her.

"What, that easily? You haven't known me two weeks and you trust me already?"

"Have you heard of intuition?"

"Yeah, of course."

"Well, I have it. You won't turn out to be trouble."

"Be careful not to trust me too much. I *am* trouble." We started to walk toward the ticket stands, and I walked close to her and whispered in her ear, "Can you believe, all this wealth and oil, and we only have this one small stadium big enough for forty-five thousand? And it's called the 'People's Stadium.' I guess that's what's they think of our people."

"Yeah, but we're at war. There are priorities."

"What about before the war? Wasn't the oil national-ized in '73? The funny thing is that this stadium was built by an Armenian who was the middleman for the oil companies. His name is Kolbinkian, but they called him 'Mr. Five Percent.' They say he's the one who built the Mustansiriyya University, too."

"Where did you get all of this information? I should be afraid of you."

"I heard it from an Armenian by accident. Don't be afraid." She pointed to the left and said, "*Zayn*, look at that Indoor Arena over there, wasn't it built during the war? Don't you know it was built by one of the most famous architects in the world?"

"Really?"

"Yes, a French architect won the bidding. My father's an architectural engineer." I was about to say to her, "Of course, we build with one hand and make war with the other," but I didn't want to alarm her too much. Plus, we had already reached the ticket stands. She wanted to pay, but I refused, telling her that it was enough that she drove us there. When she insisted, I told her that she could pay for snacks, or coffee after the game. She agreed, smiling. I thought it was a good excuse to win more time with her.

The stadium looked like a military barracks. The Tawari` forces were in full regalia, with machine guns and police dogs. Some were supervising the lines of people and others were taking tickets and searching people. Most of them were from the areas surrounding Tikrit, from the sound of their accents and their severe faces—but this was perhaps a result of their harsh training. Because this section was expensive, and because it seated the sports officials, they were more organized and less violent than they were in the cheap section, where they would use their batons on the spectators and release the dogs to frighten them. I would always laugh secretly and tell myself that we had indeed progressed far enough to be equal to European countries, where people pay exorbitant fees to go to sadomasochism clubs in order to beat or be beaten. Here the state pays the salaries of those who beat us, and we pay to enter this surrealist carnival. My grandmother would always chide me and tell me that I should stay at home and watch the matches on television, instead of exposing myself to their abuse. But the television only shows the important matches. "What are these Zawra´ doing? They've rotted your mind," she'd say.

"I don't like dogs," she whispered, so no one would hear her.

"Don't be afraid. They're tame," I told her sarcastically.

The soldier didn't dare search her, and satisfied himself by looking into her handbag. Then he said to her, with uncommon sweetness, "Go ahead, sister." Areej took two steps forward and waited for me. He started to search me with mechanical movements, climbing from my armpits to my waist and then up my back to my shoulders. Then he passed his hands over my chest pocket and grabbed the newspaper I had carefully concealed in my inside jacket pocket. When I told him that I hadn't read it yet he answered testily, "Newspapers are forbidden."

Then he threw it into a can where other papers were burning. Arguing with him would have been dangerous, not to mention fruitless. Areej didn't understand why they were confiscating newspapers. I lowered my voice as we climbed the stairs to the seats, "So we don't sit on Him."

"And burning Him is better?"

I thought about the waste of paper, and the decree that had been issued some time before, warning people not to throw newspapers in the trash because photographs of the Leader appeared on the front page every day, and people used discarded newspapers to wrap up food and clean windows, among other things.

"If they knew what happens to some newspapers," I said, laughing.

"What happens?"

"I'll tell you later."

We had entered the stadium, and the cheering got louder. "Zawra'! Zawra'!" I decided it was better not to expose her to my obscenities too early, and wait to tell her that I broke the law on a regular basis, taking revenge on the regime in my own personal way. Whenever there was a toilet paper shortage we were forced to use newspapers, and I would always choose the front page—crowded with photos and inaugurations—as a substitute. I reversed our fortunes: I would be the one sitting on the throne, and he would become the sat upon, his thick mustache buffing my anus. Of course there was always the possibility, even if it was a remote one, that a nosy trash collector would discover clues to my crime. Therefore I decided to be careful, and began to send the Leader (and sometimes his guests too) on a free tour of lower Baghdad, saying my farewell with a stream of water. We all knew the tradition of spraying water on whoever leaves us, in order to ensure their safe return!

Most of the seats were occupied, but we found two empty ones in a strategic position overlooking the middle circle. Over time the seats filled, with the exception of a small corner of the stadium behind one of the goals. Flags of visiting teams, the Asian or International Football Association, would be raised. Some genius had decided that a large mural with the Leader's image should be raised facing the field (perhaps so that he might also watch the games), thereby preventing anyone in the seats behind it from seeing the field. I would always look at that island of empty seats in the middle of a sea of forty-five thousand people and wonder if anyone would ever be brave enough to suggest taking down the mural in order for more people to enjoy the game. But those seats would have to wait for a coup or revolution in order for spectators to return to them, or perhaps they would just wait for the picture to be changed.

Rashid was leading the league, but they needed to win and get the two points in order to keep their lead. And Zawra′ gave the Rashid players a psychological complex. The first half ended with Zawra′ scoring a goal that made the crowd dance, and then in the second half the referee began to loosely interpret the rules of the game. He gave Rashid a penalty kick, but their striker missed. The referee also denied a clean goal to Zawra′, claiming the kicker was off-sides. The crowd began to jeer. But Rashid succeeded in scoring a point in the last moments and won the game.

I am now thinking of your lips, and how they caressed the ice cream that we ate in the break between the first and second halves. I can almost hear your laugh after I told you that the Iraqi Academy declared that we should use the term "creamy cold things" in Arabic instead of the English "ice cream." And how you asked me if the men wearing the suits that were spread out among the seats were "them." She didn't let me see her to her house that day, but gave me her telephone number to invite her to the coffee I had promised her.

After a night when the sounds of airplanes and gun-fire mixed with my nightmares, making me think I dreamed a war, Ahmad came in. It was the first time he had visited me since he gave me the papers.

"I came to tell you. It's over. There was a coup yesterday, and the tyrant left for Libya and requested asylum. A group called "Free Iraq" took power and granted a general amnesty for all prisoners. Get ready to leave. I'm going to go try to arrange your release—you might be able to see your family today." He embraced me warmly and kissed me on the cheek. "Congratulations, to all of us. We deserve it!"

I didn't believe him. I had hundreds of questions, about the recent developments, about the papers he gave me. I wanted to thank him, but he stopped me and said, "I hope we can sit down and have a long talk some day. I want to read what you wrote, if you don't mind, of course, but I have to go tell the others now." He promised he would visit me one day, and laughed: "Not here, of course."

"Of course. Thank you . . . very much."

"No need for thanks. God keep you."

"God keep you."

I felt a happiness I had forgotten all taste of. I thought of Areej and my grandmother. They would be glad too.

Some of them were glad, but others were nervous and scared—perhaps thinking of their own fates. The news had bestowed on them a rare amount of humanity and patience, and they allowed me the longest shower of my imprisonment—I stayed for a half an hour under the warm water without anyone screaming at me. I was afraid that it was all a dream, so I turned off the hot tap, thinking that perhaps the cold water would wake me. It didn't. Dandruff had colonized my head, so I scraped my fingernails along my scalp until my skin almost peeled off. I gave the loofah free reign over my skin, trying to scrape off the piled-up pain and filth with the foam of the clean-smelling Ghar al-ʿIsa soap. How did they know this was my favorite brand? I wished I could clean my soul as well, but it was too deep for the water to reach. They gave me a razor and some "Adam" shaving cream, but I refused to shave my beard to make up for all of those university days when they forbade me from growing it (afraid that we were members of the al-Daʿwa party or the Muslim Brotherhood). I sometimes wished that I could tell them that I was Christian, or that anyway, I wasn't religious, but what would be the use? They gave me a small mirror (how generous!), and I was surprised by an Ottoman face staring back from behind my beard. I was only missing a fez. I finished by brushing my mustache with the comb they had given me. I was pleased with my newfound appearance of dignity.

They gave me new underwear and a set of used

clothes that were too big for me: a sky-blue summer shirt, a pair of black pants, and tennis shoes. I asked about the books and papers I was carrying when I was arrested, but they said they didn't know what had happened to them and promised that they would look for them and contact me if they found them. I asked where Ahmad was so I could thank him again, but they said he was busy and wouldn't be back until the next day. They gave me my identification card and a paper with a purple stamp that proved I was among those who were pardoned.

One of them opened the door and told me that if I walked in a straight line I would find an exit at the end of the street. General Security had spread, I saw, and swallowed many of the homes that used to surround it.

Before I left, I passed by the main security post where a guard sat listening to the radio. I was surprised to hear an announcer's voice that sounded just like Ahmad's.

Everything outside the gate was calm; there were few cars in the street. I could see two columns of smoke rising in the distance from the north. A cold wind kissed me coyly on the cheek, as if to welcome me back to Baghdad's streets. The same wind ran ahead to mingle with the branches of the tall trees on either side of the street, and they answered her with a delicate rustling. A simple idea came to me at that moment: isn't freedom the most beautiful feeling in the world? Simple, trivial, everyday freedom. I didn't even allow the "No Walking" sign stabbing the grass to spoil my mood. How beautiful it was to walk without being slapped down by walls. I looked for the sun, but it was hiding behind tall buildings. I hadn't known the depth of my love for it until I was deprived of it. I crossed the street and decided to take a taxi home, the sooner to hug my grandmother and kiss her hands.

There were no taxis! I walked longer in search of a car. I saw the pages of an old newspaper running in front of me, the Leader's face fleeing, carried by the wind. I thought that this happiness might be more than my grandmother's heart could bear. I should call her first. No, I will call Areej and tell her that her love helped me stay alive, and ask her to go to my house and prepare my grandmother for my return.

The mural in front of General Security was scarred with paint, and someone had drawn horns on the Leader's head. I smiled and breathed deeply. How many times had I dreamed of a day like today? Where is he now, I wonder? Is he still smiling his feeble-minded smile? What will they do with him? Written on the walls were "Revolt, revolt Baghdad" and "If the people choose life, fate will succumb."

I looked for a pay phone. I found a stall near Songbird Records where Areej and I used to go to shop for music. All of the stores were closed. My heart danced as I thought of Areej—I longed to hear her voice. But when I reached my hand into my pocket I remembered that I had nothing. My disappointment doubled when I saw that the telephone was broken and the cord was split in two. I continued to walk toward al-Andalus Square. I raised my hand in an attempt to stop a car speeding by, but it ignored me. Who is going to stop on a day like today? I saw some red buses parked near al-Andalus Square in front of the Jacobian Church, and remembered that my grandmother would insist on calling it by its old name, "Za`im Square." And how she would praise al-Za`im. One day he left his house to go to his office at the Ministry of Defense, but he never made it. No news, nothing. The whole world was turned upside down looking for him. They were afraid something happened to him. They looked and looked for him, and do you know where they found him? He was sitting there drinking tea with the workers doing construction at the tomb of the Unknown Soldier. Why did they have to go and tear it down? It was really beautiful. I agreed with her that the new Unknown Soldier monument built near the palace was as ugly as possible. Will this one also be destroyed, or will it be moved to a museum commemorating our miserable years? Maybe I can catch a bus to New Baghdad and walk from there. The driver might let me ride for free if I showed him my release paper. But when I reached the buses I found them empty and locked, and so was the rest of the station. It would take an hour and a half to walk home from here. I would beg for the money for a telephone call if I saw another human being. I began to feel tired, and the pain in my lower back returned. I sat on a bench at the bus stop, thinking of what I would do (t)here. This is my last sheet of paper. When will Ahmad come again? I'll ask him for more. Yes, I want to write more. Maybe I can ask him to call my grandmother and Areej to tell them that I'm (t)here. They'll shut off the lights soon. Where are you, Ahmad?

ADDENDUM

According to the instructions found in directive number 234758J dated 23 August 1989, I have inspected the enclosed manuscript in its entirety, added the diacritical marks and transcribed it. The text appears to be a record of the unrelated thoughts and illogical recollections of a prisoner.

I have deliberated over the manner of rendering the frequent profanity occurring in the manuscript, but have preserved it as it occurs in the original text despite the abundance of detestable images and profanity used by the writer to deride the sayings of our Father Leader (may God preserve him), the values and achievements of the Party, and our just battle with the tyrannical enemy. This could help to identify the writer and anyone who facilitated this disgraceful transgression.

I have added margin notes in several ambiguous places to indicate what the author of the text could have intended, and added the dots and punctuation. Some of the dialogue was written in local dialects as well as the Christian dialect, and one of our Christian brothers helped me to render this. The script was generally extremely deteriorated and difficult to make out, making it impossible to read some of the enclosed pages, but I have maintained the pages in the order they were received.

With utmost respect and esteem,

Talal Ahmad
1 September 1989

Sinan Antoon was born in Baghdad in 1967. He is a poet, novelist, and filmmaker. Antoon studied English literature at Baghdad University before moving to the United States after the 1991 Gulf War, and did his graduate studies at Georgetown and Harvard, where he earned a doctorate in Arabic Literature in 2006. His poems and essays (in Arabic and English) have been published in leading national and international journals. In 2003, Antoon returned to his native Baghdad as a member of InCounter Productions to co-direct/produce *About Baghdad*, an acclaimed documentary about the lives of Iraqis in post-Saddam occupied Iraq. He is currently an Assistant Professor at New York University, where he teaches Arabic literature and culture. For more about Sinan Antoon, please visit www.sinaan.com.